THE CLAN
OF MIST

Krysta Lyn & Johnna Dee

This is a work of fiction. Names, characters, places, and incidents either are the product of the author's imagination or are used fictitiously. Any resemblance to actual persons, living or dead, events, or locales is entirely coincidental.

To request permissions, contact the authors
at info@alstroemeriapub.com

Hardcover: 978-1-959356-01-1 | Paperback: 978-1-959356-00-4 | Ebook: 978-1-959356-02-8

First Paperback Edition: December 2022

Edited by: Alstroemeria Publishing
Cover Art by Krysta Lyn
Cover Flats by Carl "Dutch" Dutchin

Physical books printed by Ingram spark and Hero and Villain Designs.
alstroemeriapub.com

To my friends and family who always encouraged me to think, dream, believe and dare to create. - Krysta

To all those who supported me, made me laugh, and made me cry I thank you. -Johnna

The Clans:

The Clan of Mistbright:
Crocodile and amphibian shifters
hold the Amulet of Earth

The Clan of Skye:
Halcyon water birds
hold the Amulet of Wind

The Clan of Eldritch:
Local vampire hoard
hold the Amulet of Darkness

The Clan of Helbram:
Fae and Nymphs
hold the Sun Amulet

The Clan of Elzora
Witch covens
hold the Amulet of Fire

The Clan of Ulrich:
Wolf shifters
hold the Moon Amulet

The Clan of Thalassic:
Sirens
hold the Amulet of Water

Chapter One

Thessalia's dark hair floated on the water's surface, hiding most of her pale skin. Her almond-shaped hazel green eyes were filled with dread as her heart shaped face bobbed on the water's surface. It had just turned midnight; it was officially her 13th birthday.

Thessalia sat there peeking above the surface of the water, watching her mom. Talora sang a song so hypnotic, so soft and so gentle. Her jet black hair hung down her back. Thessalia watched as her mother's hair curled around her with the whipping of the wind. Her pale oval face shone in the soft moonlight. The pale gray slip dress barely covered her skin, her pale legs looked fragile peeking out the bottom. She stood on a rock a mile away from shore. Her sultry brown eyes were locked with the sailor's. Hips gently swayed back and forth in a hypnotic ritual dance that had been passed down through generations. Her hands waved in a rhythmic motion, enticing him to come closer and closer.

He brought his boat, drifting directly towards where

she stood. He was a small, fragile-looking male. Alone in a small fishing boat, probably from up shore somewhere. Thessalia was curious what his village was like. Were other men like him? How did his voice sound? What did he smell like? Her nostrils flared at the thought, her nose filling with the scent of the musty sea breeze.

The sailor's eyes never left Talora's. He was already under her spell. Thess knew it was too late for him.

She reflected on the first time she watched her mother perform the ritual to the sea Goddess Amphitrite a year ago. She knew she would see that night, in her nightmares for the rest of her days. Thess didn't think she would ever be able to do this. No matter how many times they made her watch. No matter how many times they told her it was her duty and how it would make the clan stronger for future generations to come.

She closed her eyes, knowing what would happen next and not wanting to watch before she dove below the surface. Her teal fin glinted in the moonlight that filtered through the shallows as she made her way back towards her village on shore. Out of the corner of her eye, dodging between strands of seaweed, she saw her friend and cousin, Nementeia, swimming away from lessons as well. It gave her comfort knowing she wasn't the only one who didn't want to watch.

From a young age, sirens were taught what their duties were and how to act, move, and breathe. while singing their siren song. How to seduce with a note, with a glance, with a gesture. Every time when someone came close to their village since her twelfth birthday, she had attended these lessons. Only during one of the solstices were they allowed to have a day of break from lessons.

Her mother, Talora, was the leader of their clan

Thalassic, and she was heir to the clan. Talora was always telling her how important it was that she take her lessons seriously. The legacy was to be passed on to her and she was required to continue the tradition. Her mother had held onto it for two-hundred years. Before that, her grandmother and her mother before her. For generations, the women of her bloodline held on to the matriarchy and power by shedding the blood of their enemies and anyone who opposed them. The expectation for her to do the same scared her down to the core.

She had heard the stories of the battles since she was a baby. Over and over again, her responsibilities of duty and leadership were drilled into her head.

She made it to shore before the others arrived. She started the transformation back to her legs. The scales sloshed off, turning into dust as her skin tore through. Her fin broke apart and separated. Her legs twisting and breaking back into shape. The webbing transforming back into her feet. It was just a blink of the eye, but there was a moment of genuine pain every time she changed. Bracing herself in the shallows until she could wobble to shore. She sighed as the pain faded. She loved both her forms, but that brief moment always made her wonder what it would be like to just choose one.

The others were coming back. Her mom was upset and she could see it.She watched the teal fin, the same shade as her own, break apart and twist into legs. The scales fading away as skin broke through. Talora stood up and walked to the shore like it was nothing at all.

"Thess," Talora scolded. "One day, you will lead this clan. If you neglect your lessons…"

So many times, she heard the speech so many times that she knew it by heart. She felt she could never live up to her mom's expectations. Wasn't sure she wanted to live up to them. She wasn't sure she could lead a male to his death…

The next morning, Thessalia was woken up by the commotion of her mom moving in the next room. She tried to curl deeper into her bed. The nightmare from the night before still plaguing her waking world. When she closed her eyes again, she could see the rain pouring from the sky in sheets. It was the first night she saw what her mother really could do. The ocean turned and churned around her mother's feet as she sang the haunting lullaby of the siren's song. A lullaby that lured a vessel towards the danger that lurked just barely below the murky depths of water and sea foam. The lightning flashed illuminating the deck, but the male's face stayed in shadow, his dark hair whipping around his face.

That night a year ago, she had seen her first male. The first night of watching her mom do the siren's call. Nothing had been the same since then.

Inhaling deeply, she took a few calming breaths, trying to shake off the nightmare. She was not ready to get up and start the lessons. She wanted to have one day for herself;one day of freedom to see the world outside their village and the nearby town. Would one day even be enough? A taste of freedom she would only have once in her life.

She could hear her mother coming down the hall in their small shared house towards her room. The rising sun was barely cresting to cast a pale golden glow on the curtains of her room.

"Thess, get out of bed now," Talora said, sternly coming into her room without bothering to knock. Her mother slapped her foot that was dangling off the edge of the bed before turning on her heel and heading back out.

She groaned as she stretched and then slithered out of bed, going as slow as possible. Her mind ran back to the male last night.

Her mind wandered further to the male who had sired her. Wondered how much like him she was. Her face and eyes were nothing like her mom's. She didn't have her personality. She was already taller than Talora, who was a dainty 5'2. She was a lanky 5'6 already. She wondered if she looked like her dad. Acted like her dad. Did she have his smile? His laugh?

Thess made her way into the kitchen where her mother was drinking a cup of tea and looking out the window towards the ocean. She looked at her mom, knowing the answer, but asked anyway. "Mom, what was my dad like?"

Talora looked towards her, frowning before turning away. "How should I know?"

Throwing a piece of bread on the brasier above the fire, Thess turned to add more water to the kettle to brew some tea for herself. She sighed at her mother's curt answer because that is how it always went. She never answered any of the questions she had about the male who sired her. A siren seduced a male, took his seed, then…

"I think you need to be reminded why we do this," Talora said, disrupting her thoughts.

Ugh, Tess thought, not again.

"Come," Talora said, holding her hand out for her daughter's.

Thess sighed, dumping the half-toasted bread onto a plate before grasping her mom's hand as they walked out the door towards the Temple. So much for getting in some warm sustenance before her lessons.

Their clan owned the small section of Florida beach for the last 200 years. Small houses with no electricity. All the houses matched. A sandy brown color that sat on stilts. Designed to blend in with the land. Most had two bedrooms, a living room, kitchen, and a bathroom.

The town sat by the ocean. A simple village, currently inhabited by thirty-three sirens. They were one of the bigger clans of sirens in the Western Atlantic .

As far as the eye could see, was their small community of homes, rocks, shore, and ocean. Rarely did anyone come this way unless lured. No roads led directly to the village. No shipping routes went here. There was a small parking lot over 2 miles north up the beach, but no one in the village owned any form of transportation. Except for Thess, she had been given Dromie's old beat up car when Dromie was gifted a new car by her uncle. No one knew about the car since they never traveled that way.

They were completely isolated. It made her feel so alone.

She only had her one friend and cousin Nementeia, in their village to spend what little free time she had with. They were the two youngest sirens.

Thess always wanted to go explore what was beyond their village, to see the world. Her curiosity of the world was so strong. Older sirens would tell her gossip about the outside world. She would sit there hanging onto every word.

She knew her mother would never allow her to leave the village. As daughter of the clan leader, she was to stay here and set an example of the dutiful siren. The future clan leader.

She watched other sirens walk by them. Taking a deep breath, she geared up for the speech for the millionth time. She knew every word that would be said, every gesture that her mother would make.

They arrived at the Temple just as the sun started rising higher. The Temple was tucked into a small alcove in the hill that shielded the rear of their village. Its green marble columns gleamed in the morning light shining through the cave entrance. Four pillars on each side, for the four elements carved into each. Fire, Air, Earth, and Water. With water marking the center pillars. They crossed the threshold. Sconces that had magical blue flames were on the walls, lighting up the room. It illuminated the room in a soft blue light, making the room feel like the bottom of the ocean the way the light danced around. The sigil for water was carved into the green marble flooring. The amulet of water sat nestled inside. No furniture, just the amulet on a pillar. It was surrounded by six guards at all times. One way in and one way out.

Or at least that is what most thought. Her mother had shown her the secret passage. Only three people knew of it; herself, her mother, and the high priestess, Asiris.

There were seven Amulets - water, fire, earth, wind, sun, moon, and darkness. To protect them, seven clans were blessed to each guard an amulet. Legends told that the amulets were to never be reunited. They were never to cross the threshold of the Triangle either. Her clan was the guardian of the water amulet.

The Clan of Mistbright, crocodile and amphibian shifters, held the amulet of earth. The Clan of Skye, the water birds, carried the amulet of wind. The Clan of Eldritch, a local vampire hoard, retained the amulet of darkness. The Clan of Helbram, nymph and fae, carried the sun amulet. The Clan of Elzora, witch coven, possessed the fire amulet. The Clan of Ulrich, wolf shifters, guarded the amulet of moon.

The blue of the center of the water amulet shone so brightly even in the dim lighting of the temple. It seemed like it glowed with its own magical light from within. The teardrop blue diamond was nestled inside a silver filigree that swirled around it like waves. Little blue diamonds set inside the silver waves. Thess had always been drawn to the amulet. She could feel its power churning inside, waiting for her, calling to her. Its song so gentle and quiet but ever-present when she was near it. Sometimes she dreamed she could feel and hear it in her dreams.

Instinctively, she reached out to touch it. Her mom smacked her hand away, breaking the soft trance she had felt.

"You know better," she chided. "The only time you will ever be granted to lay a finger on the amulet is if you win the tournament and take your rightful place as leader." She grabbed Thessalia firmly by the elbow, forcing her to turn and meet her eye to eye.

"For two centuries," Talora started. "Our clan has fought to hold on to the amulet from the other siren clans and any others who would try to possess it. I have led our clan to numerous victories in battle. Our bloodline has fought in the tourneys and won for centuries. In nine years' time, you will have to fight and defend our reign of the triangle and the amulet. You need to take heed of your lessons and…"

Thess knew, no matter what, she would never be ready to fight and potentially kill the champions of the other three clans. Every twenty-five years, they held a tournament. The two clans would meet on a guarded island near the Bermuda Triangle. The individual clans chose their champion. Usually, the choice fell to the shoulders of the leader of the clans or their strongest warrior. Whoever's champion won would be guardians of the water amulet and of the Island until the next tournament.

The Bermuda Triangle was a vortex of magical powers. Home to a demon that had slumbered for eons. The seven clans fought hard to lock away the demon so he could not destroy the earth again. Many people have tried to explain the anomalies that happened around it. If only they knew the truth of our world.

She had been told the stories of her ancestors, her mother fighting in the tourneys every twenty-five years. For the last two-hundred years, Talora Potamides has ruled. Her mother ruled through her strength and determination. However, she kept saying she was ready to step down and let Thess become the leader of the clan. In nine years, when she would be twenty-two, it would be her turn to fight and lead the clan.

"I know…" Thess muttered, squeezing her hands into fists at her sides, feeling her magic rising up at her change in mood.

"Thessalia," Talora said, gently. "You are not like the rest. You must be stronger, faster, smarter. You are to rule the clan one day. You must start acting like it."

Thess tamped down the frustration and rage bubbling up inside of her. She had given up on fighting, there was no winning the battle with her mother.

As she parted ways with her mother, leaving the temple, Nementeia ran up to her. Her long blonde hair trailing behind her, bouncing around her shoulders with each step. Her warm brown eyes shone with laughter as she slipped an arm through her own and turned them towards the destination of their first lesson. She always had a genuine smile on her face. No pretenses.

"Are you ready?" Nem said, hurriedly. She was always rushing around and never sat still for long. "Miss Z is training us on vocals today. She is so much better than Miss Kaleigha. Way nicer... Did you hear about Deandre? Kaia saw her..."

Nem talked all the way to vocal lessons. Thess wasn't sure when she even stopped to breathe. Listening to Nem go on was always weirdly peaceful. Plus, somehow, she always knew the latest gossip. Maybe it was because Asiris was Nementeia's mother. The high priestess knew all, viewed all... or something like that. From birth, they were destined to be friends due to their stations. She was always thankful that Nem made it so easy to be friends.

Miss Z stood at the front of the class. Nem was right, she was a lot nicer. Miss Kaleigha would not allow little things to slide. Miss Z didn't constantly criticize her posture by whacking her in the back. She didn't scream "From the diaphragm" in her ear. Plus, she gave her less tedious lessons in comparison to Miss Kaleigha, who would give her double the lessons.

Some days, she just wished they wouldn't expect so much of her. The expectation to fight harder, sing louder, be more enticing was not something she wanted. She wanted to blend in and be herself. She just wanted to be like everyone else, but that was never going to happen...

Chapter Two

Present day, Cape Sable, Florida

"Come on Thessalia, we are going to be late if you don't move your land loving legs faster!" Andromeda proclaimed, while jumping up and down. Her multicolor curls bouncing around her shoulders and her dark eyes staring insistently. Dromie's pink sparkly dress hugged her curves perfectly. Her matching pink heels were sky high. Her best friend was a Halcyon, a water bird shifter from the Clan of Skye. She wouldn't trade her for the world, but she had the patience of a squirrel.

Smiling, she reminisced about the first time she ever met Dromie. Thess had been fourteen years old when she first snuck out of her village. She had wanted to see what was beyond there. While exploring through the everglades, she had gotten lost trying. She wasn't sure where to go or how to get back home. The scent of the wet grass seemed to be all around her. Then there she was, appearing out of nowhere. Standing before her was a bouncy, multi hued, curly headed breath of fresh air. Dromie had helped her find her way back to her own village. Never expecting anything in return for her generosity. Luckily, Talora never found out, at least not that time that she snuck out. They had been the best of friends ever since. Inseparable.

"Calm down, Dromie. We all can't just fall from the sky looking fabulous." Thess finished putting a layer of pink gloss on her lips before snapping closed her compact mirror and stashing it in her purse. She glanced at her reflection in the bathroom mirror critically. Her gold bodycon dress curved around her form. Shining in the light. She had cropped her dark hair, to her mother's annoyance, to just below her shoulders. The layers framing her heart-shaped face just right. She used shiny gold and black eyeshadow to highlight her hazel-green eyes. Her black satin heels shined in the bathroom light.

Training had been nonstop for the siren tourney happening in two weeks' time. She could recite her siren songs in her sleep, forwards and backwards. Pushing her body to its physical limits over and over. With her years of training, she was as ready as she would ever be for the tourney. She was nervous, thinking about the tournament and its impact on the rest of her life and her clan. She could feel the nerves building up inside her, bubbling up like the frothy sea foam in a storm. Fear of letting everyone down ate at her.

She hadn't taken any time for herself lately, focusing solely on her training. When Andromeda invited her to go out with some of their friends to a local club where magical creatures could mingle with humans without being detected. Most could pass themselves off as human, but the few who could not had special charms and spells to appear human.

Thess figured it was time she relaxed. What could it hurt to have a few drinks and dance. Just take a moment to forget who she was, and what she needed to do for one night.

Talora would be furious if she knew she was missing out on any time to prepare. She just had to make sure her mother didn't find out. She had been extra vigilant about the tourney coming up. Her mother rarely let her out of her sight. She would freak out if she found Thess snuck out, let alone went to the club.

Thess took a deep, steadying breath in. It was just one night to relax. She needed the time away, or else she might break. Her whole life may change based on the outcome of the tourney.

The full moon shone brightly, illuminating their path as the pair walked down the sidewalk from Dromie's apartment. Their heels clicking, the buzz of insects and the rustle of the breeze through the palms as they made their way inland. The ocean air wafting on the wind to her nostrils. She heard the club before she saw it. She always loved to see the bright lights of the club.

The Wave was the hottest club in Cape Sable, Florida. It was always packed with humans and magical creatures alike. Wards from the local witches prevented the humans from seeing those who couldn't shift into humanoid forms.

The line to get into the club wrapped around the building. A mix of humans and magical creatures mingled in the line. Two large wolf shifters stood at the door's entrance checking ID's and letting people in. They jumped in the VIP line, going straight for the doors that the bouncers opened, their biceps bulging to let the girls in without batting an eye. Andromeda's uncle, Faulkner, owned the club and she was a frequent visitor at night, and helped him during the day when the club was closed. The beat of the music engulfed Thess the moment she walked inside, her heartbeat speeding up to pulse in time with the beat. Closing her eyes, she took a moment to let the music surround her and lost herself in the moment.

They made a lap around the dance floor, saying hi to old and new friends. Dromie introduced her to some unfamiliar faces that she hadn't met before. The dance floor was packed. It seemed like there might be magical creatures from all the clans there tonight. There weren't many places that catered to all the Clans and magical races. Some Clans were very territorial. Somehow, Dromie's uncle, Faulkner, made it work.

Dromie always seemed like she knew everyone, and those she didn't know became friends with her instantly. Her smile always lit up the room. Her laugh was infectious. Where Thess tended to be a bit more reserved, shy. She had trouble approaching people she didn't know. They were completely polar opposites in personality.

They decided to order a drink and chat before hitting the dance floor. She ordered a Death in the Afternoon cocktail. The sweet bubbly combination of champagne, simple syrup and absinthe always made her relax and lighten up her mood. She slowly took the first sip. Chasing the green fairy. Feeling the slight burn go down her throat and warm her insides. The glorious feeling you get after a few sips when it swirls in your head. She felt the rush of lightheadedness, that spinning feeling.

She listened to Dromie flirt with Nix, a green witch from the local coven. His unruly wavy blonde hair swirled in the air conditioner breeze. His light brown eyes crackled with the magic he held behind them. He half-heartedly listened to her. His eyes scanning the room behind her.

Dromie twirled a pink curl of hair around her finger as she sipped from her flute of pink dragon spritzer, batting her eyelashes at him. Her dark eyes glanced up at him longingly. Doing anything she could think of to try and get his attention.

Her friend had been crushing on him since they were kids. She could not figure out why a water bird could fall for a witch. Her friend was a powerful creature and, combined with her personality and wit, she could have anyone she desired. She didn't know why she wasted her time with Nix, a run of the mill green witch. He always seemed like he was distracted and never gave Dromie much mind. But, Dromie was an eternal optimist and kept trying. She was always telling her about life mates and hoping one day to find hers. She had nearly convinced herself that Nix was hers if he would only just be open to his feelings. Life mates were two souls that were destined to be together through fate. She would tell her that an individual could go their entire life without ever finding their mate but when they would, it was a bond that went deeper than physical need for each other.

Thess was unsure she believed the stories Dromie would tell. They seemed as much of a fairy tale as 'love at first sight'. Plus, she didn't even know if sirens could have mates or if being mated was only for other magical creatures. She laughed quietly to herself thinking that it would be a cruel trick of fate to give a siren a mate when they were destined and trained to lure, use, and discard males.

Lost in her thoughts, Thess continued to consume the bubbling green liquid, reminiscent of the inland pools of swampland. She could feel the beat of the music reaching into her soul. Her hips began to sway in time to the tempo. Finishing her drink, she set down her empty glass on the bar and moved her way onto the dance floor.

A tall male slid up to her side. His scent of deep, rich, and woodsy permeated her senses, marking him as a wolf shifter.

"Care for a dance, beautiful?" He flashed her a grin before he started swaying to the beat with her. She thought his name was Theo. They met once or twice before.

"I bet you say that to all the girls." She purred back, falling into the rhythm of the music. His hands rested on her hips as they swayed in time together. She felt the length of him next to her body. The lights flashing. The bass thumping. For a moment, she forgot who she was, where she was, and what she had to do. She just let herself be lost to her senses, lost in the tempo.

The song ended, the rhythm changed and broke the spell she let herself fall into. Smiling up at the male, the shifter's attention had already left as he turned to dance with a wood nymph. The nymph's aura of magic surrounded her as she gyrated with him. Her hair swaying around her body like the branches of a weeping willow blowing in the wind.

Turning in the other direction, she left the dance floor. She scanned the room to find Dromie, spotting her up near the VIP section. She had lost Nix and was talking to someone Thess didn't recognise. Dromie smiled at her as she approached, grabbing a full cup of golden swirling liquid from their table and handing it to her.

"Finally, having fun and letting loose Thessie? It's

time to celebrate. In just a few weeks, you're going to compete in the trials and show all those sirens how much of a badass you are." Andromeda's eyes twinkled as she gestured to the tall blonde male standing next to her.

He smiled, his vampiric canines glinting in the lights of the club. "Thessie, meet Trace. Trace, meet Thessalia. We were just talking about how exciting it's going to be to see the competition this year. Trace was telling me how ruthless your mother was when she first competed, and her mother before her."

Thess halfheartedly smiled at her friend, thinking about the lecture her mother had given her earlier about not disappointing her. She closed her eyes for a second, pushing the thoughts away. Tonight was about relaxing. Not thinking about her mom or the tourney. She took a large drink from the cup she had been given and made a face as it burned all the way down her throat.

"What is this?" She grimaced. She sat down at the table with them and swirled the liquid in the cup watching the gold dance and move like the currents in the ocean during a stormy sunset. It left an aftertaste of burnt sugar and fall sunsets in her mouth. Her head instantly started to feel bubbly and light again.

"My uncle's new bartender is testing out recipes to liven up the menu. She's a friend of Nix's from his coven. Apparently she comes from a long line of herbalist witches, but she enjoys making cocktails more than healing potions. I hear her clan isn't super impressed and threatened to disown her if she didn't focus more on their family's heritage. You know my uncle, not one to leave a stray out in the summer heat. He opened his doors and gave her an opportunity," Dromie said, absentmindedly. "I want to try them all to see which I like best. This is the Ginger Gold Rush. You don't like it?"

Before Thess could answer, Trace lifted his gaze from Dromie to nod to the bar. "She's even managed to add a few things to the menu that are palatable to our tastes, although nothing beats drinking right from the source and animal blood just doesn't have the same potency."

She looked into his cup of dark red liquid, a chill running down her spine, and she lifted her cup in cheers toward the two of them.

"To each their own, I suppose?"

The others raised their cups in cheers. She took a big gulp. Let the alcohol slide down her throat, warming her from her soul to the tips of her toes.

The waitress, a swamp nymph, walked up to the table. "Anything else you needed, Miss Andromeda?"

Thess looked at her name badge, Cordewai. Thinking she might be new. She didn't remember seeing her before. She had turquoise colored hair. Her bright green eyes sparkled in the dim lights.

"I would love to have another Pink Dragon Spritzer, please," Dromie said wistfully. Resting her chin on the palm of her hand. "Do you guys want anything else to drink?"

Before Thess could say anything, the doors to the club opened and closed. A warm breeze with the slight hint of the sea and swamp filled her senses. Suddenly, she was overwhelmed by the scent of sweat and perfume wafting through the club.

She felt his eyes on her before she even saw him, goosebumps flushing across her skin. Her breath caught and her heartbeat increased. The whole world seemed to be quiet at that moment, as the only thing she could hear was the rhythm of her heart in her ears. Something about him was captivating. His black hair fell across his forehead and one eye haphazardly. Skin tanned and sun-kissed like he had spent hours out in the sun. Eyes that were black pools as dark as midnight.

For a brief moment, their eyes locked across the dance floor. Her breath caught as she could not avert her eyes from his. She felt herself get lost in the dark depths of his eyes. Her body flushed from a heat burning inside her. She bit her lip as she felt her heartbeat speeding up inside her chest.

She had never felt like this before. Her senses felt more alive and in-tune with her surroundings, yet at the same time, he was all she could see, smell, or feel.

His gaze swept from her feet to her face before meeting her eyes again, piercing into her soul. She couldn't look away. Then he turned and vanished into the crowd. For a moment, she felt a sense of loss.

Chapter Three

K age strolled briskly into the nightclub. The smell of
sweat and alcohol hung in the air. The lights flashing
to the beat of some song he didn't recognize. He surveyed
the room, looking for his target.

He just wanted to get in, get the job done, and get out.
They needed a bit of surveillance before they completed
the last deed. The information they obtained would give
him insight into what he would have to deal with. Find
out what his target was like so that he could formulate the
eventual plan.

This was the last job that bastard demon would make
him do before he got his family land back. Bring his clan
back together. The clan Mistbright. He was almost free.

He saw her sitting at a table across the club. Just a
glance as he quickly looked her up and down, assessing.
Their eyes locked for a moment. He felt a heavy weight
drop to his stomach and a strange feeling. He quickly tore
his eyes away, shaking his head.

It was just nerves; he told himself. He walked to the

bar to shake the feeling off. Except, when did he start feeling… nervous? He'd been taking jobs for as long as he could remember so he could try to climb out of the hole his father had buried their family in. Working his way through any means possible to rebuild what should belong to him and his clan. It must be the excitement of the finality, the glimpse towards a future he never let himself imagine. A future with his homelands and estate under their rule, out of the thumb of the tyrant water demon, Azazel. He occasionally snuck onto his family estate. The ruin and neglect would make his mom cry.

He couldn't wait to never deal with that demon again. The demon had summoned him with his offer to give it back if he paid off his father's debt with interest. He had become a lethal weapon ever since. His natural predator instincts of his ancestors' ability to shift into a crocodile kept him alive.

Freedom was in sight. He couldn't get distracted now. He had to stay focused on the job at hand.

He brushed his black hair out of his eyes. His dark, hooded eyes surveyed the room. A scar slashed across his face from a fight long ago with another shifter. He stood just over 6'2", able to peer across the entire crowd as he continued to survey his surroundings. His bulky muscular physique stretched his shirt tight across his barrel chest. Moving from the bar, he skulked around the edges of the room, like the crocodile shifter he was, letting his senses reach out around him. His skin was tan, his hands rough and calloused from hours spent outside, working out on various jobs. He clenched his fists, closing his eyes as he leaned against a wall in the corner, waiting.

He remembered when he was young and his father would drag him to the secret underground

gambling den that was below his feet. Faulkner ran
the den below the club. He could barely make out
the outline for the hidden door that led down to the
basement. He walked up to the bar and ordered a
WereWhiskey. Neat on the rocks.

There was a time he had looked forward to
coming here. Seeing the lights, hearing the music,
meeting the people. He remembered when his father
would bring him here to watch him play cards. Watching
the few winning hands was exciting. The hope of
another winning hand, addictive. The anger and
frustration that came when he inevitably lost... That
time was long gone. He hated this place now. It was a
tragic reminder of what a fucking bastard his father had
become.

It was where his family had lost everything. At least
almost everything. He toyed with the intricate key that
hung off the necklace around his neck.

It was a calm, balmy night when they came to get
the bastard from The Wave once again. Kage was just a
scrappy eight-year-old. His mother, Hana, had dragged
him here several times before to collect his father. He
thought it would be just like any other night, but it
wasn't.

He remembered his mom opening the secret
passage door. The musty smell of cards and cigar smoke.
There were three tables, a waitress running around
delivering drinks to the patrons. As soon as they walked
in, it went quiet. Their footsteps sounded deafening as
they walked to where his father stood. His father stood
next to a demon. It was the first time he had seen a

water demon. Heck, it was the first time he had seen any demon, for that matter.

He looked up at Azazel. He remembered the first time their eyes met. In the water demon's ice-blue eyes there was no emotion, just like staring at death. Cold and calculating. Chills ran up and down his spine. He didn't know this was only the first time of many. He would have to deal with the icy bastard. The demon extended his hand, and they shook. His hand was clammy and cold, almost lifeless. One thing he could say was the demon never treated him like a child, unlike the others.

His gray hair slicked back, not a strand out of place. His pale, almost gray, skin was almost translucent. He wore an impeccable white suit. No wrinkles, no spots. He looked like a true southern gentleman, but colder, crueler.

His father, Jameson, would not look at him or his mom. He just stared at the ground, shifting back and forth nervously. His hands fidgeted with the buttons on his old worn out shirt. His scraggly brown hair hiding his eyes.

"What did you do?" his mother, Hana, said. He heard the quiver in her voice, the fear. He looked at her with uncertainty. Her black eyes glistened with tears. Her black hair slicked back in a ponytail. Her facewas paler than normal.

That's when it hit him. This was not like all the other times. This was much worse. No matter what happened, she was always calm. But not this time. It scared him to see his mom like this.

His father just stood there. Still refusing to make eye contact.

"Jameson?" she said louder. Tears started running down her face. The fear rising in her voice. Kage felt the knot grow bigger in his stomach as he watched his mom.

Azazel's smile grew bigger and colder. A slight laugh escaped his mouth. "Your dear husband has just handed over the rights to all your land. I expect immediate evacuation from my property. Immediate. Have a great day, folks." His southern drawl made Kage's skin crawl.

He walked away. No cares of the destruction he had left in his wake.

"I was doing so good," Jameson started, still fidgeting. Never looking up. "But that bastard had to have been cheating. No way he could have beat me otherwise. Don't worry, I will fix this. It is just a temporary setback."

Hana threw herself at Jameson. "You gambled away my family's land? How could you?" she screamed. She was beating her fists on his chest. After a while, the rage had left her. She fell to the ground, sobbing. Kage went over to hug her.

Jameson kicked him away. "Mind your business, boy."

"Maybe, you should mind your own business!" Kage screamed, defiance shining bright in his dark eyes as he stared at his father, torn between wanting his old dad back, the one who taught him everything he knew, and being disgusted with the foul sniveling creature he had become.

Jameson backed handed Kage. "How dare you speak to me like that, boy? I should have taught you respect sooner." Jameson took another step towards Kage.

Hana jumped between them. "I'll take care of him."

She planted her legs squarely, waiting for the first blow. But, it didn't come. Jameson stared at his wife wondering when she had finally grown a backbone. Since the first day her father promised her to him, she had always backed down. She never stood up to him. Never.

Kage reached his hand up to touch his cheek, still hot from the sting of the back hand he received across the face. He felt the blood drip from his lip. His face throbbed. He would never forget this. It was the last time he would let his father lay hands on him or his mother. This would be the last night his father ever made his mother cry. He would make sure of it.

He stared defiantly at his father. Making sure the old man saw all the rage he felt. Daring him to come after him with all the false bravado he could muster. Jameson looked from mother to son. Shook his head. Then turned and walked away, head hung low.

Hana stood there for a moment, unsure of where to go or what to do. She reached for her son's hand and started the walk back to their home. At least the place they used to call home.

As they climbed the stairs, he could hear everyone start to talk again. He heard his mother's name said several times. He looked up at her. She looked devastated and dazed.

They went and grabbed what little they could take from the house.

"Grab whatever you need that can fit in this suitcase." Hana said to him.

He remembered her grabbing a small chest. She cradled the chest lovingly. He had never seen it before tonight. She handed it to him gently, lovingly.

He looked at the plain, dark square wooden chest. A small intricate lock was the only decoration it had. It looked like it could never possibly hold anything of value. Old, scarred, and beaten up. He stared in confusion at the chest.

"We must, at all costs, keep this safe! From your father, from everyone!" She said fervently. He had never seen her so adamant. No matter what beatings she took, she remained calm. Except for tonight. She was not acting like the mom he knew. "Everyone! You can never tell anyone about the amulet. We must keep it a secret."

She stared at him for a minute. Her eyes begged him to understand. He stood there, eyes shifting from the box to his mom. Processing her words. Trying to figure out what she wasn't telling him.

"Do you understand me?" she asked with more urgency.

Kage nodded.

"No, say it out loud. Swear it. Swear you will protect the contents of this box with your life," she said intensely.

"I swear, mama," he said solemnly.

She stared at her son for a moment. Reading his expression. Making sure he understood how important it was that he keep this promise at all costs.

She brushed his hair lovingly out of his face and kissed his forehead. As they packed, she acted like his old mom again.

They took the small chest and the few clothes they could carry. One last time, he looked back. He had never lived anywhere else but in this house. The tears welled up in his eyes. He brushed them away, trying not to let his mom see his sadness.

They walked miles and miles in the dark swamp land with nothing but the buzzing sound of the insects, the lapping of the swamp water on the mangrove roots and the light of the moon to guide them to Lorairia's house.

As they walked, he felt a calm come over him. The

smell of the swamp was always comforting. It was the only home he had ever known. The feel of the breeze blowing through his tousled hair. He quietly walked next to his mom.

He could see the tiny shack of Lorairia's coming up. The candle-lit windows were a beacon of hope. They walked up to the shack. Lorairia opened the door, having smelled them coming.

Luckily, Lorairia took him and his mom in without hesitation. Hana and Lorairia were the best of friends.

When his dad vanished, no one was surprised. He had not seen him again since. Not sure if the old bastard was dead or alive; he didn't even care whether he was or not. Not long after, his mother, Hana, got sick and died. Reminding him of his promise once again on her deathbed. Telling him that their clan had been the guardians of that chest for hundreds of years. She gave him the key to the box. A key he wore on a chain around his neck.

Lorairia raised him as if he was one of her own. Her son, Griffin, became his brother. Together, they roamed the swamps.

One more gig, then his mother's land and estate will be his again, he reminded himself. Kage would fix what his father had destroyed. Would set right the wrongs his father had done to their clan. He would make everything right again. Watching the girl for a few days would give him the intel he needed. First, he needed to formulate a plan to take her. Exchange her for the amulet. Then, give Azazel the amulet, trading this last job in exchange for his family's rightful lands. Easy breezy, right? What could possibly go wrong?

Chapter Four

Kage surveyed the room. Just then, Kage noticed Griffin heading towards him. He sidled up next to him at the bar. The cocky son-of-a-bitch was already buzzing from the look and smell of him. His step was a bit off-kilter as he threw his arm around Kage's shoulders. He could smell the WereWhiskey on Grif's breath as he leaned on him.

"So what's the game plan?" Griffin asked, causally. Glancing over his shoulder, scanning the room. Kage assumed he was looking for her.

"Just observe and nothing else." Kage said, quietly. "We are here for intel only. Try to be a little less obvious, please. By the way, how much have you had to drink tonight?"

Grif laughed, winking at Kage. "Enough."

Kage shook his head in annoyance.

"Can't we just take her now?" Grif said, whining dramatically. "Just get it done and over with. Then, we can go have some real fun. I know a nymph or two I can introduce you to. Plus, I bet I could get her to follow me right out those doors willingly."

Grif winked exaggeratingly and raised up an arm, flexing in his friend's face. Kage stared at him in annoyance, a low growl emanating from the back of his throat.

"You are no fun at all." Grif said, then proceeded to order another WereWhiskey for them both. They waited for the bartender to walk away before continuing the conversation.

"Last time I let you talk me into doing something impetuous, we ended up in jail cell in bumfuck. Not going to let that happen again. I'd prefer to play this by the books," Kage laughed, a half-smile spread across his face. "Plus, I am so not interested in your cast offs, even if there are two of them."

"Are you sure?" Grif said, grinning. "I can vouch for their skills."

Kage stared at him for a moment before shaking his head.

"There's a lot on the line," Kage said, turning serious. His smile fading away. "We need to keep it clean and simple. Do what's best for our clan. Think you can do this?"

"You know I can," Grif sighed. His eyes turned serious as they met Kage's.

"Get lost and sober up. You know what's at stake with this mission," Kage told Grif, shoving him away with a huff of annoyance. He knew he couldn't stay mad at him for long. He never did. Grif was the closest thing to a brother he had. He watched as Grif walked away to go talk to a group of people he knew.

Grif was a sore thumb no matter where he went. His baggy jeans hung a little too low and his tight white shirt stretched across his stout chest. Faded old brown leather cowboy boots on his feet. His black hair and amber eyes caught many girls' attention. He thrived on all the attentiveness the girls' provided. Constantly would go out of his way to get noticed by them. He was a snake shifter, practically a genuine snake oil salesman. He could charm the pants off an eskimo in a blizzard and had done so to the ladies on many occasions.

Dumb pretty boy, Kage thought with a laugh as he took a deep swig of his whiskey.

Kage grabbed his half-empty glass and moved to a recently vacated table in the corner. From that angle, it gave him a better vantage point in the club. Where he was now, he could stay hidden in the shadows, so as not to be seen by others. He wanted to observe her quietly, without being noticed.

Plus, he wanted some peace and quiet. When Grif drank, he could talk anyone's ear off. He needed to learn her habits without the distraction Grif would bring, and he didn't have a lot of time left. His time was running out to construct a plan. There was a lot that needed to be done and not much time to execute it based on the timeline that the water demon had given him, two weeks. Two very short weeks.

He looked around the room. He found her still at the same table with two other magical creatures, talking and drinking. Loud music blasting on speakers through the club. Humans and magicals roaming around.

Thessalia. He rolled her name off his tongue a few times. The next leader in line for the siren Clan of Thalassic. Daughter of the famed siren, Talora Potamides. A vicious family of siren's known to tear a male's heart out before he could blink. They had what he had been challenged to collect as the last test from the water demon for him and his clan's freedom. He watched as she brushed her dark hair off her cheek with an elegant sweeping motion.

She seemed like she wasn't paying attention to the conversation going on around her; like she was distracted. She kept nervously glancing around the room, searching. He wondered what it was she was looking for. Turning her eyes back to her companions, she laughed at something one of them said. He watched her tongue dart out to wet her lips. Something stirred deep in his core. Shifting in his chair to get more comfortable.

One of the magicals sitting at the table was a vampire named Trace. He and Grif would go out drinking from time to time. They had a competitive streak with one another over the attention of the ladies.

The other person sitting at the table was a halcyon. The halcyon was doing most of the talking from the look of it. He thought she might be related to Faulkner. He had seen them together, from time to time, running around town.

He went to sip his whiskey before realizing it was empty. He motioned towards the redheaded waitress for another one. Sitting back, he crossed his arms across his chest, just observing them as he waited for the bartender to bring over his drink.

As the waitress walked away, out of the corner of his eye Grif caught his attention. Grif had stood up from the bar and slithered right up to the group in the VIP section. Kage felt his gut tighten.

"That slow witted cretin," Kage muttered. He slammed his fist down on the table. "He's going to blow this up to hell and back."

Kage debated if he should go stop Grif or stay where he was at. He gripped the table, his body rocking forward, opening his senses to hear over the roar of music and voices. Unfortunately, he could not discern their voices from all the others around. He started to stand up, but the bartender dropped his drink off on his table. He sat back down, fuming. Taking a long drag of his whiskey, to tamp down the anger.

Grif stood between the halcyon and Thessalia, his back turned to Kage. If only he could see Grif's face to see what the dumbass was saying. He didn't have time to fix any fuck-ups Grif might be creating.

Thessalia lifted her eyes again. She had not been able to find the mystery man again. Eyeing all the surrounding faces, she searched for him all over the bar, and he was nowhere to be found. She did, however, notice that behind Andromeda, someone was approaching them. Her eyebrows furrowed in concentration, trying to think of where she had seen him before. A nagging feeling of recognition, but she could not recall where she had seen him before.

"Tall, dark and handsome coming our way, Dromie. Is he one of your friends?" She put a slight emphasis on friends while giving her a wink. While Dromie only had eyes for Nix, she had scores of males vying for a moment of her attention.

Dromie turned to greet him. The shifter leaned on the table between Thess and Dromie. He was grinning from ear to ear like a kid in the candy store.

Kage breathed a sigh of relief when after a few minutes of talking, Grif guided the halcyon onto the dance floor. They danced for one song before separating, and Grif walked away.

He was going to murder Grif for pulling this stunt when he saw him next. What the fuck had he been thinking? Kage wondered. Thess didn't act suspicious or nervous, though. Hopefully that meant Grif didn't go fuck anything up and at least learned something that they could use. Kage had his doubts.

He watched Thessalia the rest of the night. Taking a note of what she was drinking, who she danced with, who she talked to. His eyes stalked every move she made.

She accepted the invitation to dance with a male witch. The pendant on his chest marked him as the clan Elzora. He watched her hips sway with the beat of the bass when she danced in sync with him. Her hands swayed gracefully. The witch's hands rested on her hips. He felt a twinge when he saw the witch's hands move on her hips. Kage's eyes were glued to her. She had hypnotized him.

All night, she kept stopping and looking around randomly. Obviously, she was searching for something or someone. His eyes scanned around, trying to figure out what she was looking for. He would watch as her eyes surveyed the club, following the directions her eyes took. She obviously was not finding what or who she was looking for because her eyes continued their search occasionally.

Around a little bit before two in the morning, she decided she was ready to leave the club finally. She started to make her way to the exit, hugging a few people as she slowly headed to the doors. Stopping to gab to some other people. Then she eventually walked outside.

He followed her from a safe distance. That way, he could watch what path she took home. Stealthy, quietly stalking behind her. She didn't even look back once. Her eyes just watched the sky as she strolled to her car.

He jumped on his Harley Sportster to follow her, keeping a gap between them. The breeze felt wonderful on his skin as he drove the winding road. Watching her car tail lights as her car hugged the curves of the road. She pulled up to her parking spot away from the town. He turned his bike off a distance away and rolled it up towards the parking lot.

He stayed close to the shadows. No one was outside. The lights in the houses were dark, the town was quiet. She also stuck to the shadows, sneaking around stealthily. She was obviously trying to not be discovered. If he hadn't been watching from the start, he might not have noticed her.

When she got to her house, he watched puzzlingly as she walked around the house before she climbed in through a window instead of going through the front door.

Why would a twenty-two year old climb through the window? He puzzled.

As she got ready for bed, he could see her silhouette through the curtain. As he watched her, he felt a stirring inside him. He closed his eyes and took a deep breath, trying to focus on the task at hand. He needed to get his head on straight.

"Focus," he mumbled to himself.

This job might be easier than he thought. She would make an easy target, completely unsuspecting. All he had to do was lure her away from the water so her powers wouldn't work, and quietly get her away from her clan. He just needed to come up with the plan now.

He brushed his hand through his hair in frustration.

He sat there for a while after she had turned the

lights out, a lot longer than he needed to wait.

Chapter Five

Thess woke up. Those eyes had been haunting her dreams. His dark, deep, rich as the shadows of the bayou eyes. She couldn't stop thinking about the stranger she had glimpsed briefly in the club, their eyes connecting over the crowd before he had disappeared. She had searched for him throughout the night, but could not find him. There was something about him that had drawn her in…

She shook the feeling off. Pushing herself to the edge of the bed, she got up before her mom could come in and harp on her. It was time to get up and prepare to do her lessons.

A quick glance around the room and she spotted her shoes cast in the corner, a few dresses tossed haphazardly over the back of a chair, and her favorite brush on her nightstand. She was ready to go by the time her mom entered her bedroom, barely pausing to knock.

Time to go practice her siren songs. It was another day of endless training. She felt her mind dragging a bit. She had stayed up too late and had too many drinks. Taking a deep breath, she stretched before yawning and running her fingers through her hair. It had been worth it. She felt more relaxed today.

Miss Kaleigha was giving her lessons alone today. She would prefer anyone but her to train with. Miss Kaleigha was no nonsense. There was only one way to do things, and it was the way she taught you.

Miss Kaleigha's brown hair was slicked back in a tight bun. Perfectly coiffed, not a stray hair out of place. It was as stiff as her personality.

Thess always felt like a mess compared to her. Her hair was thrown up in a messy ponytail, a few strands falling around her face. She quietly obeyed, trying to hide how tired she was from the night before.

"Time to start your breathing exercises." Miss Kaleigha said. She started the metronome.

Thess closed her eyes and listened to the beat. She started with her breathing exercises in time with the clicks of the metronome. She put one hand on her stomach, just under her ribs, the other on the top of her chest. Sucked in the air, counted to 20 with the metronome, then exhaled. Breathe in through the nose, hold, then release through the mouth.

This was one of the few things that she liked about the lessons. It was such a relaxing exercise and helped her feel the balance between her breath, body, and magic. She could release her tension with this exercise.

Miss Kaleigha walked her through all the breathing exercises. When they were done, Thess felt more centered, more relaxed.

They moved on to the next set of exercises. She looked down at the bowl of water in front of her and listened to its song, the way the water lapped the edges of the bowl.

She was tasked with creating a minor storm in these waters. A lesson designed to help her control her song spells.

She felt the song rising up inside her. Listening to the voice in her head going over the siren song again and again. She could hear the voice, her own voice, the soft lilt. She let it swirl through her before she slowly started casting the siren spell out loud. Her voice gently sang out the spell.

Οι δυνάμεις του νερού, οι δυνάμεις του αέρα, αυτή η σειρήνα σε καλεί σε σένα, Το νερό αληθινό μπλε του νερού στέλνει παλιρροϊκό κύμα Όπως θα είναι τόσο mote είναι.

Keep it small, keep it focused. Just in the little bowl in front of her. She could feel the storm brewing in the bowl. Feel the splash of the water when it overtook the edges. Hear it as it crashed against itself. She kept casting the spell. Over and over.

"That's enough, Thessalia." Miss Kaleigha cut through her concentration, already moving to whisk away the bowl and motioning for her to move on to the next bit of training for the day. That was the one she dreaded. They wanted her to do it in the ocean; in front of everyone. She hated the fact that everyone was going to just be staring at her, judging her.

The thoughts were still spinning in her head when she realized Miss K had cleared everything up and was standing by the door. The lesson was over. Now, it was time to go outside and show off her true potential. She had done this dozens of times. Just usually it was her and the teacher or her mom, Talora.

She took a deep breath. Tried to block everyone out.

She looked down at her bare feet. Curled her toes in the sand. Then slowly ambled to the ocean. She kept her eyes downcast. Trying to forget the crowd staring at her.

"You got this!" Dromie cheered. Thess looked up at her and half-heartedly smiled.

She felt the gentle waves lap onto her feet as she stepped into the ocean. She tried to block everyone out. Closed her eyes, took a deep breath; let the world slip away. It was just her and the salty water. She was now waist deep. She opened her eyes and stared into the vastness of the ocean.

The water was calm. Gentle waves pulsing, nudging her. She closed her eyes. Heard the spell in her head. Let it simmer for a moment. Inhaling deeply, and then started the siren's song.

Οι δυνάμεις του νερού, οι δυνάμεις του αέρα, αυτή η σειρήνα σε καλεί σε σένα, Το νερό αληθινό μπλε του νερού στέλνει παλιρροϊκό κύμα Όπως θα είναι τόσο mote είναι.

She felt the water swelling up around her. Using her voice, she controlled every drop of the brewing storm. She felt so alive at that moment. Her body and magic embracing the ocean's power and sharing control. She was no longer nervous. The eyes of the crowd no longer affected her. It was just her and the brine.

She continued to sing as the surrounding storm around her grew bigger and bigger. She sat in the eye of it, marveling. Feeling her hair being whipped around. She opened her eyes. Watched the eyewall whip around her as the sun beams scattered through the waves, casting shards of broken rainbows for only her to see. Sitting in a calm in the middle as the brine raged around her. She felt her voice grow stronger and clearer.

She sank into the feeling. The power of the hurricane that she had called, shaped and created. It sang to her bones, her very core. Her lips drew up into a smile as she marveled at it and herself. She was amazed at the strength in her spell and the thrill that coursed through her veins letting her magic free.

She calmed her voice, changing the spell song.

Δυνάμεις του νερού, δυνάμεις του αέρα, αυτή η σειρήνα καλεί, Φέρτε αυτόν τον τυφώνα. Σε όλους τους ωκεανούς μπορείτε να περιπλανηθείτε, φέρτε αυτή την καταιγίδα σε μένα! Γιατί κιθ και συγγενείς είσαι για μένα.

The water slowly calmed, drifting around her body until it returned to the rhythmic push and pull of the tide. She heard applause from behind her. Jarred from her reverie, she remembered that she was not alone. Her pulse quickened as she turned around. The nerves came back as she took in the faces of the entire clan.

Dromie ran into the water, cheering. She grabbed Thess up in a big bear hug.

"I knew you would be great!" Dromie yelled.

"I wasn't sure if you would come, or if they'd let you watch," Thess replied breathlessly.

"High tide, nor your mother could have kept me from supporting you. You are my best friend!" Dromie said excitedly. "I am here for you and will be there at the tourney, too!"

Nem raced up right behind Dromie, jumping up and down.

"You did wonderful!" Nem said, excitedly. "You are so going to win! I have never seen such a big storm in such shallow water!"

Thess blushed from the compliments. Other sirens continued to compliment her performance, leaving her with words of encouragement as the trio made their way towards the shore. Even Miss Kaleigha nodded approvingly from the shore.

She avoided her mom's eyes for as long as she could. Fearing what she would see in them, disappointment. She straightened up, pulled her shoulders back, brushed her hair out of her face.

She met her mom's gaze.

"Not terrible," Talora said sternly, her arms crossed across her chest. "You still need more practice. Your tone was quite weak at the start and you didn't gain as much power as you could. You need to hold it steady throughout. Every misstep or weakness you show is a liability."

Talora turned and walked away. Thess grinned. That was the nicest lecture she had ever heard.

Dromie grabbed her cheeks. "We need to go get lunch and tell me about how it felt!"

"Yes, please," Nem groaned. "I am so hungry. I could eat a whale."

Dromie laughed. "We should go stop at the new burger joint. I'm told the food is great. I've been wanting to try it."

The three of them walked to Dromie's car, parked as close as Talora would allow any vehicle or road to come. She listened to Dromie and Nem telling all the latest gossip they had heard.

They drove the many miles to the burger joint. The food smelled so fragrant. Her stomach growled as she remembered she hadn't eaten since last night. She had been so busy; she had forgotten. The feeling of being drained hit her, between staying up late and casting spells.

Plus, starving, she thought as her stomach growled.

Grabbing a table inside by the open patio doors, where they could smell the sea breeze lazily drifting by, they ordered their lunch.

As they waited for the food, Dromie said, "we should start planning your victory party. Of course, we will hold it at The Wave. My uncle will let us have the place for the night. We need to figure out the theme, what we are wearing. Are we going to have it the day after we get back?"

"What if we did a gold theme?" Nem suggested. "We can all dress up in all gold. Gold decorations and have the new bartender create a gold themed drink menu."

"Oh, and then we could…"

Thess zoned out as Dromie and Nem planned a party for her. Listening to them calmed her nerves. They were the best friends anyone could have had. Always so supportive.

They already assumed she would win and planned accordingly. She wished she had as much confidence in her own abilities as they had in her. She was not as sure she would win this battle as they were. Sometimes though, when she felt the magic coursing through her veins, she felt invincible. When the water swirled around her she felt free and in charge.

The waitress delivered the food, a bacon cheeseburger, and fries. She picked at the fries on her plate as she listened to them talk about the party.

She had the feeling she had when his eyes were on her last night. She shook her head, willing the feeling away. It was all in her head. Thess swallowed, not sure how to approach the subject.

"Last night at the club…" she trailed off as a warm sensation slowly traveled down her spine, causing goosebumps to pop up on her skin. Her cheeks blushed.

"Yes?" Dromie asked.

"There was a shifter. I hadn't seen him before. Dark eyes, black hair, had a scar across his face. Do you know who he is? I… I had not seen him before and was curious…."

"I'm not sure I saw him at all." Dromie said, her curls bouncing as she shook her head. "Rings no bells. I can ask around."

"No!" Thess yelled. "It's not that important. He's probably someone from out of town visiting a friend, most likely. I need to be keeping my focus on the tournament first, not getting distracted by strangers"

She wasn't sure what she was feeling or why. No need to have Dromie tell everyone she was looking for him. Best to keep it to herself. She didn't have time for this, anyway.

Chapter Six

Kage watched Thess from a safe distance. Making sure he stayed upwind of her and the other sirens, that way, no one would catch his scent. It had been a little while since he had last tracked someone.

Reminiscing about all the times he had been hunting in the swamps when he was a kid. One of the few wonderful memories he had of his dad, learning how to scout while in and out of his shifter form.

He watched her leave her house and stroll into another. Every once in a while, he would catch a slight glimpse of her through a window. The sky blue slip dress she wore left little to the imagination as she swayed while she practiced her vocal lessons.

He had never heard a siren's song before, hoping he would never have to hear one. There were too many stories and legends of sailors, both human and nonhuman, falling into their trance. Many men died after just hearing but a few notes from her kind. He was going to make sure he was not one of them, he told himself as he slipped a pair of magical sound dampening plugs into his ears. They were specially made to not hinder one's hearing, but dampen audible magic.

Thessalia came into view once more. One hand was on her stomach, the other on her chest. Her pale skin stood out against the blue of the dress. Watching her chest rise and fall with the deep breaths she was taking. He closed his eyes and imagined it was his hands on her instead. Moving out of view again, he lost sight of her. Feeling the disappointment wash over him, pushed it aside, while she was out of sight.

A bead of sweat traveled slowly down his spine. Glancing up towards the sun, he noted it wasn't even noon yet, and it was already hot and muggy outside. He had found a bit of shade to hide under, but it didn't make it any cooler. He glanced around the village. There were twenty-five small homes, a few sirens walking around. The ocean tides rose and fell, playing with the sand. The village was mostly quiet, except for the muffled sounds from inside of the houses and the occasional siren talking.

A giant gray and brown rock wall was at the backdrop of the village. Creating a wall of shelter behind it, with the open blue ocean waters on the other side. The middle of the rock face had a small opening. From his angle, he could not see much of what was inside.

Two sirens entered the crevice. They looked like they were guards. A minute later, two other guards left laughing and joking, their voices too quiet to understand the conversation from his distance. This must be the changing of guards.

This is most likely where the Water Amulet was held, he thought. Too close to the water to fight off all the sirens'.

Thess drew his attention back to the house she was in. She had come back into view again. Her hair falling out of her ponytail as she bounced in and out of his view.

Pacing back and forth in the shade, he brushed a hand across his hair as his sweat dampened his brow. Dark hair clung to his forehead. He was used to many scouting missions, but from where he was stationed, he couldn't feel the breeze coming off of the ocean, blowing the palm trees scattered throughout their village and down the beach. Reaching into his pack, he grabbed his water canteen and took a swig, grimacing at the stale, warm water. Continuing to watch, his eyes tracked her every move when she came in sight through the window. He needed to know what she was like and how she reacted so he could plan accordingly.

She stayed inside the house for a few hours while he stood watch. The blue of her dress made it easier to see her when she was in view of the window.

He had thirteen days left to make a plan, prepare, and execute it. That was not much time to work with, he thought to himself.

The siren tournament would happen and there was no guarantee the amulet would still be within his reach. That was a hard rule Azazel had given him. The amulet must be his before the tournament.

He was exasperated by the time the door opened. She waved goodbye to whoever was inside and finally left the house. Sweat beaded his brow, his shirt clinging to his chest. He watched as she confidently waded into the cool blue ocean. When she was waist deep, she stopped. Transfixed, he sat there, thoughts of his uncomfortable state leaving his mind.

For a moment, she stood still. Then she opened her

mouth to sing the siren song. He could not hear the spell she cast, but he could see what it was doing. Her hands moved, guiding the water that was swirling around her. It started slowly at first, then it picked up speed. It came faster and stronger than any storm he had seen before. The swirling waters soon surrounded her, as they grew till he could no longer see her. Wind was whipping and slashing violently while the mixture of white, blue and teal water rushed around her body, shielding her in the middle of the miniature hurricane. The ocean around her thrashing against the sand. A few sirens stepped back to get away from the violent winds surrounding the hurricane. Then she released the spell, the water slowly going back down and gentling. She stood for a moment before turning to the cheering crowd.

It was only a few minutes, but it felt much longer. This just reinforced why he needed to make sure when he kidnapped her, she was far from a body of water and kept her away from it. If he let her cast a spell with the water, they would be in a world of hurt. This was the time he had ever seen a siren of wield water magic before. The way she just did with such ease showed she must be an extremely powerful siren. Even the strongest crocodile shifter he knew who had some control over the swamp water could not do what he just witnessed her do.

Slowly, she came out of the water. Her dress was clinging to her skin. He could see every curve, every arch, all of her outlined in great detail. A breeze blew, causing her thin blue dress to flair out behind her. He felt his heart speed up in his chest as he admired her. He adjusted himself, trying to push the thoughts away and concentrate on the mission was there for.

There was something about her. He just couldn't put

his finger on it. It was easy to just watch her, too easy for him. Even miles away, he knew he could pick her out of a crowd. He brushed his damp hair out of his face in frustration.

She started heading towards two women who were waving at her from the village. One of them was the halcyon that Grif told him about, who was named Andromeda. She was all smiles as she greeted and hugged Thessalia.

The other appeared to be another siren. He did not know her name, yet. However, she was likely related to Thess based on their similar features. Her blonde hair swirled around her as she bounced up and down with excitement. They spoke too fast for him to read both of their lips. The obvious excitement radiating from them both. Thess stood quietly, a shy smile spread across her face.

The group of them stopped occasionally to talk with other sirens. Then finally Talora spoke to them. He knew that was a siren he did not want to mess with, especially after the rumors he had heard. Talora had a reputation of ripping hearts out with her bare hands before her victims could blink.

They continued to walk along the path, which would leave them just past where he was stationed. Backing up into the trees, he crouched, letting his magic roll over him, changing his tanned skin to the green, brown hue of his crocodile form without fully transforming so that he blended in better.

As they walked by, he heard them discussing the restaurant they were going to for lunch. He had heard of the restaurant, so he knew where they were going.

After they were a respectful distance away, he stood up and shivered as he let his reptilian skin fade. He pulled his motorcycle out from the shrubbery where it was hidden, making sure his bag was cinched down tight. He kept his distance as he jumped on his motorcycle and followed them into town.

Parking his motorcycle down a nearby alley, he casually strolled out and continued to follow them, keeping them within earshot. As they walked to the burger joint, he listened as they talked about the tourney. He found a bench across the street from the restaurant. He pulled his baseball cap down some more and tilted his body, peering at them from beneath the rim.

They were sitting at a table by the open doors, talking and laughing. Between the noise of passing cars and other conversations happening around them, he couldn't tell what they were talking about even with his enhanced hearing. With their heads turned, it was difficult to read their lips as well. He was debating if he should go in and see if he could hear what they had to say. Or if it would be better to just stay here and continue to monitor her whereabouts.

As more sweat dripped down his back, he debated whether he should head in or stay here. The idea of cooling off and hearing the conversation they were having was so appealing. Sitting in where it was air-conditioned. Sighing, he knew it was no contest. Wiping the sweat from his brow, he decided to head inside.

He slowly entered, making certain to stay out of her line of vision. Her back was to the door, making it easier to go by. He brought his hat down lower, side eyeing her the whole time. Tucked his hands in his pockets, he nodded at the waitress.

"Pick wherever you want to sit hun, here is a menu. The weather is beautiful out on the patio today. A slight breeze blows right through and you look like you could use some fresh air," the waitress said, handing him a menu and looking him up and down. He glanced down at his sweat dampened shirt, frowning.

Nodding his thanks, quickly walking past their group and other patrons until he was at a table at the far end of the room. He took a seat, sitting with his back towards the girls, and picked up the menu without really looking at it, closing his eyes and letting his senses open to their conversation. He blocked out the other people talking and eating around the restaurant, centering on just them. Their voices carried over to him.

The waitress came over to take his order. Deciding to order coffee and a sandwich while he sat there listening to them chatter. He wanted something quick and simple. That way, he didn't walk out too long after them. Munching the sandwich and occasionally sipping his coffee, he eavesdropped on their conversation.

He listened as they praised her for her skills today. Talked about a party when she won the tourney. They were going to have it at The Wave. Discussing different themes. Thessalia stayed quiet for most of the meal. Andromeda, aka Dromie, as she was nicknamed and Nem, the name they called the other siren, did most of the talking. They seemed so excited to plan this party. Both were talking extremely fast in their excitement.

Half heartedly he listened to them talk as Thessalia sat quietly. His ears perked up when she mentioned looking for a shifter. He sat there intently listening to her soft voice. Trying to hear each word around the din of the restaurant. Her voice trembled with nerves.

Looking back he tried to remember if she had

danced with another shifter, but she had not. Maybe it had been before he had gotten there. Choosing her next victim, he thought with a huff. He rolled his shoulders and a frown crossed his brow.

She stuttered out the words. At first, he didn't believe his ears, then it hit him all at once. She had mentioned a scar. His scar. His heart stopped for a moment and he froze. He looked over his shoulder to see if his ears were deceiving him. Why would she be asking about him? He wondered, as his heart started racing.

Chapter Seven

Thess got back after eating lunch with Dromie and Nem. She had thought that afterwards she would feel rested, except that she didn't. Her heart felt as restless as an electric eel. Her mind was overflowing with anxious thoughts spinning around. The rest of her body felt drained and tired.

She walked further down the beach, avoiding the places where she knew her mom could conceivably find her. She needed a moment to be by herself. Not sure where she was going or what she was going to do. Wandering around a bit aimlessly. When she looked up, she was standing in front of the temple. The columns gleaming in the light of day. She stood there a moment, staring at them.

Unconsciously she had walked here, or maybe she was just pulled here. A bit of magic calling to her and guiding her.

Taking a deep breath, she entered the temple. Glancing around, she saw the six guards at their stations. They stood around the amulet, surrounding it, backs to it, ever guarding it. The guards changed every three hours, in groups of two. That way, a new set of guards was there, who were always rested and alert.

A few of the guards looked up at her as her footsteps echoed off the sandstone floor. Stopping in front of them.

"I need a moment of meditation with the amulet. Can I get a bit of privacy?" She said, with all the authority she had.

They looked like they wanted to bulk, but she just stared all of them down. Standing up taller, pulling her shoulders back, to appear taller and more intimidating. They walked outside the temple one by one.

She sighed the instant they left. Knowing that they were just outside the threshold, but for now, she had a small bit of privacy. All members of their clan had access to enter the temple. It was a sanctuary of peace that stood in honor of the Goddess, Amphitrite. The sea goddess who protected all living creatures of water. She had watched over and protected their clan for ions. There was no better place to host and protect the amulet prized by all siren clans.

Her mother had never let her touch the amulet before. The amulet was to be watched over and never touched. Wondering if her mother ever came to admire it even, she doubted it. Doubtful her mom even held it between the tourneys. She didn't know when the last time it had left the pillar even was. Most likely when the last tourney had been held, twenty-five years ago.

Closing her eyes, she could hear the amulet singing to her. A siren song of its own making. A gentle lullaby that grew louder and stronger the closer she got to it. The song had drawn to her for as long as she could remember. Wondering if her mother and the others could hear the lullaby the amulet sang? Was she the only one that felt that pull, heard that song, was drawn by the call? Her whole life it had called her. She had wanted to talk to her mom about it but her mother always brushed her questions off. Just as she did when she asked about her father.

She admired the sparkling blue of the diamond teardrop. Its inner flame burning bright in the dim light. The gleam of the silver waves glistened in the candlelit room. She could not resist reaching out and gently caressing it. This was the first time she had ever touched the amulet. The first time she had ever been alone with the amulet.

A jolt of magical electricity vibrated through her. The warmth spread throughout her entire body. For a second, she felt like she could conquer anything, as long as she had that amulet in her hand. She felt so much magic coursing through her veins.

She yanked her hand away. A bit frightened by the power she had felt when she touched it. She took a moment to breathe in and out. She was so startled by the magic, the emotions she felt from touching the amulet. A mix of joy and fear all at the same time rolled through her.

"For centuries, siren clans have fought over you," Thess whispered to it. "Soon it will be my time to fight. I don't think that I am ready for the tourney. My fear is that I am not strong enough, fast enough. Not even sure I would be able to finish my enemy off, if it came down to it even. I don't want to bring shame to my clan or my mother, but…"

She trailed off a moment before continuing, biting on her lip. "I have trained all my life. Almost every day there was a lesson. It feels like it still is not enough training. I can sure use some advice from you here. Just a little bit...."

Pausing, she waited with bated breath, but no answers came. She sighed. She should have known better than to expect an answer. Just that same calming sweet lullaby calling to her.

She reached over to touch the amulet again. Her finger slid over the waves, the diamond. It was so warm to the touch. She felt the power that pulsed through it, warming her up to the tips of her soul. Closing her eyes and letting it hit her in waves, the magic song playing in her head, the power coursing through her veins. She tried to hear the spell in the song, but no one had ever taught her this spell before. The words were hard to understand, so faint she could barely hear them. It was like it was a language she had never heard but somehow knew.

Maybe if she touched it, she would hear an answer to her question. She gently lifted it off its velvet cushion, just a fraction of an inch. Gently cradling it in her hands. The wave of magic washed over her. She swam in it for a moment, closing her eyes for a second.

"Any advice?" she asked, opening her eyes. "Anything at all?"

She waited, nothing came to her. No answers, just a feeling of warmth, a song she had heard many times before, and so much magic, magic she had never felt at such a level before.

Resting the amulet softly back in its spot, she pulled back her hands. Crossing her arms over her chest, she took a step back.

"I am scared," she stated. "I don't want to be like my mother, but I don't want to let her down, either. I am nothing like her, if I am being honest. But I am also torn with wanting to do my duty, honor the clan, my mother, protect you, and the triangle in our clan's guardianship. All the while getting to be like other people my age. Ones who get to choose the life they want for themselves. Get to do the things that they want to do. Not the life that is given to them. I just wish I had more time."

She exhaled deeply. "Would I ever be ready? Even if I had all the time in the world?.... Probably not."

She paced around the room restlessly. Looking at the green marble walls, the floor, and anything else for a moment. Trying to calm her thoughts and tamp down her fears.

Turning back to the amulet and walking back over to it. She stood over it, looking down at it. Wondering if her mother made the right choice in choosing her. Has her mom ever had the same doubts she had? Talora never acted like she had the same fears, the same doubts. Always seemed to be so sure of herself, so confident in what she did.

"Thessalia," Talora said sternly from the entrance to the temple.

Thess jumped, startled that she was no longer alone. She turned slowly, wondering how long her mom had been standing there. Has she heard or seen anything?

"Yes, mother?" Thess whispered, clasping her hands behind her back and bowing her head down.

"You have played around long enough now," Talora stated gravely. "You are already late for training, once again. You need to take this seriously. This is not a game we are playing. It is beyond the time that you should be at combat and weapons training. Raemeda has been patiently waiting for you on the training grounds. You have a lot to perfect in two weeks' time. Now quit screwing around and get going."

Thess sighed, realizing her mom had not heard her talking at least. A small bit of relief hit her knowing this.

She followed her mom from the temple to the training grounds. Raemeda stood in the center of the grounds, in front of a table filled with weapons. She walked over and looked down at the array of weapons. Swords, daggers, axes, you name it. Some were older than her mother, from the look of them. Tracing her hand slowly over the weapons, she felt the pulse of magic the they held. She looked at the spells carved into the blades. They had passed these down from generation to generation. She had been told a few of the tales about them, but not all, which surprised her. Curiously, she had not realized they still had relics; she had not known the tales about them.

"Today I want you to practice with the Sword of Peleus," Raemeda said intently.

This was a sword she had heard the stories of before. She picked up the sword for the first time. The sword was a leaf-shaped blade, which created a wider blade profile. It had straight cross guards. The hilt held a blood red ruby that gleamed in the sunlight. The handle was well worn and comfortable in her grip, from the grip of sirens before her. A cold strength radiated from it.

They had passed the sword of Peleus down in their clan for centuries. The legend goes that it had belonged to Peleus, the father of Achilles. He had forged it when he fought alongside Hercules. Legend says the sword grants the person who wields it victory in battle.

She had been told that it was 'gifted' to their clan when one of Peleus's heirs fell in love with a siren. She always laughed at the idea that they had given it to them.

They had probably handed it to the siren when they fell under her siren song spell.

They brought it and the other weapons over here when they had to leave their home country of Greece. They had settled here in Florida after the war, fleeing to America in search of a new start. Thess and her mother had never lived in Greece. She didn't think any of the sirens who were alive today actually lived there. This was the only home they had known.

Another thing for her to stress on. If she didn't win the tourney, how would it affect the clan? How would they handle it if she lost?

She crossed the blade a few times in front of herself. Testing the weight, the dexterity. She had never held this sword before, so she took the time to get to know it.

They started out with the basics drills. She did them absentmindedly. Thrust, cut, block. Practiced over and over repeatedly. Once Raemeda was happy with the basic drills, she picked up a sword as well.

Thess smiled with determination. Maybe this is what she needed. A good fight. She threw herself into the fight with the last of her waning energy.

Going on the offensive, she thrust the sword at Raemeda, but was blocked by the sword. She was jarred from the impact of the blades meeting. She kept pushing forward, using all her strength in every swing. Raemeda kept blocking every one of her swings as she stepped back.

Thess received a kick to her side from Raemeda. She grunted and stepped back. She could feel the bruise from the kick. They circled one another before Raemeda dove for her. She jumped to the side, turning to bring the hilt of the sword down on Raemeda's back.

She heard Raemeda grunt in pain as she fell to the sand. It gave her a boost of confidence.

They continued to parry back and forth until it was dinnertime. Thess was extremely tired. She barely touched her dinner. She climbed into bed, falling asleep before her head touched the pillow.

Chapter Eight

Kage paced around the cabin like a caged lion, waiting for Grif to show up. Of course, that snake was late once again. Sighing, Kage looked up at the ceiling, trying to find some patience.

Kage continued his restless stroll from one end of the room to the other of the cabin. He had built it after he turned eighteen. It was about a mile from Lorairia's home. Grif had a place in town he stayed at when he wasn't at Lorairia's house.

The cabin was small and nothing special, but it was his. He had worked hard to build a spot for himself here. The first floor was one big great room, a small kitchen and a bathroom. In the main room, there was a bed pushed up against one wall, while an old, beat up brown couch sat adjacent to it. Against the far wall, he had set up his computer and monitors for the surveillance equipment he had installed these last couple of days. The monitors covered the extent of the wall.

Downstairs was the concrete basement he planned on

keeping her in. He had kept it sparse on purpose. The plan was for her to not be staying a prisoner for long. The longer she stayed, the more chance he had of being caught. He didn't want to give her any opportunity to injure herself, him, or Grif with extra frivolity in the room. A table, a chair, and a bed were all that was there in the room. A small bathroom he had removed the door from and shut the water off, too. Security cameras covered every part of the room to cover all the blind spots.

He had brought in a new generator to power everything. He could hear the soft hum of it coming from off in the distance. Fixing all this up had used up his entire savings. It had to go right, he couldn't afford for it not to. He appreciated Lorairia's generosity, but he was ready to live back on his family's estate and move the three of them out of this area of the swamp. His homelands had more fertile land for them to live off.

The house had an enormous kitchen that Loriaria would love to play around in. Plus a spot for her to grow a garden of her own. Reminiscing about how great her cooking was, he missed it sometimes.

He was not much of a cook, he thought laughing, He couldn't wait for her home cooked meals.

He had snuck into the old estate house from time to time. To walk through the halls, remembering what it had used to be like in its glory days. It would need a lot of repairs, since it had sat vacant all these years. The overgrowth of plants, the broken windows and furniture. He hoped there was no structural damage. He looked forward to fixing it up and transforming it back to its old glory. He would have more free time after he finished this last mission to work on the house.

He had spent the last couple of days watching Thessalia, ensuring he could snag her without any hiccups to the plan. He had her schedule down, which was easy since she did the same thing every day. Her routine was just like clockwork. Other than going to the Wave the one night, her routine never differed.

The plan also involved devising a way to keep her without her escaping or using her water magic to hurt either of them. Grif and he had sat down for hours formulating the plan. Grif was a key part of these plans going smoothly. He didn't have an abundance of time to get this done and, of course, the bastard was late.

He looked to his right arm at his watch, watching the second hand tick by. It reminded him of the way she mesmerizingly swayed back and forth while calling upon her magic in the shallows of the sea. He felt his heart sprinting at just the thought of her. Closing his eyes, he could picture her, her wet dress clinging to her curves as she stepped out of the ocean. The heat rose in his loins.

Frowning, he shook his head. Recently, just the thought of her made his heart race.

He was becoming weak, he thought in disgust, if just the thought of a female was sending him off the edge.

Trying to shake the feelings off, he ran his fingers through his hair. It was just nerves from this last mission getting to him. It could not possibly be any other reason, he told himself.

Running his fingers through his hair in frustration, his mind wandered back to where Grif could conceivably be. That was more important than this. It shouldn't have been surprising that he wasn't on schedule. The snake was always idling his way around just to slither in just a tad bit late. Kage thought he made damned sure that the snake knew how important this mission was for him, though. He pounded a fist against the doorframe, staring down the stairs through the entrance to the darkened basement below. The steel door stood open.

Grif and himself had completely different mindset and demeanor. Where he was more serious, Grif was more lighthearted. Whereas he liked plans, Grif liked to fly by the seat of his pants. He was never entirely sure how they got along, since they were so different. Also never quite sure what antics Grif would get them into.

Kage went around the room, inspecting it, looking for flaws. He felt that something was going to go wrong and just wanted an alternative plan to handle it.

After sealing off the window to the outside, cutting off any potential communication to other creatures or water, he had picked up a dehumidifier and installed it in the basement. He wanted to suck as much water out of the air as possible. That way, she had less chance to use her siren water spells on them.

Next, he had reinforced the door frame and added a steel door with an auto lock mechanism that was linked to his and Grif's watches. As a safety measure, he had all the first floor locks updated on the safe house, for the door and the windows.

Racking his brain, trying to think of everything that could go wrong. He worried he hadn't found every Issue. Surveying everything again, looking for any flaw, but couldn't see them.

Next, he needed Grif to help him trick Thessalia into taking the potion and getting her here before it wore off. He was a bit more suave when it came down to those things, so it might be easier for him to get it to her. A bit of jealousy ran through him at the idea of him seducing Thessalia into taking the potion.

He was going to drag Lorairia into it too. It upset him to no end that she was involved, but he saw no other path. She was the only person in the world besides Grif, that he trusted, to get it done right. To also keep quiet about everything that was happening. So much depended on this working out.

He had to do this all while protecting himself, his friends, his family, his clan, and at the same time, not cause a war. That was going to be the hard part. Making sure she didn't know where or who they were. That her mother did not know who took her, either.

Making sure no one could know who they were working for. Azazel would have his skin tanned and hung from the wall of his insipid keep should he blow his cover. He could kiss his family's estate and land goodbye forever, all while creating an extremely powerful enemy.

He had procured two deep sleep potions from the swamp witch, Cassio. The witch reassured him that the potion should put any siren to sleep and curb their powers for at least eight hours. With the powerful magic that she had demonstrated while he had surveyed her these past few days, he wasn't putting his chance on time. The witch had guaranteed that she would not remember the moments before she took the potion and it would make the hour before hazy in her memory. She reassured him that the potion was tasteless, odorless, and non-detectable. Thessalia wouldn't know what was coming. They just needed to slip it into her drink without her noticing.

The witch also sold him a pathway spell to hide their trail. He wanted to make sure any track they made was cold by the time anyone realized she was gone.

This had to work and had to go according to plan. Or else…

He pulled out his phone and opened up the messages, sending a quick text to Grif.

'Where the fuck are you?'

Putting his phone back into his back pocket, he paced the length of the safe house, stopping to peer out of the window. He had double-checked that everything worked about a dozen times but still felt the worry in his guts.

Kage had her entire schedule memorized. Knew the direction they would take to avoid people. Realized who he could trust and he could not. He knew where they would meet up at. They set a timetable for everything.

Now, if only Grif would do his part and show the fuck up.

He walked outside and sat on the porch stairs. Gazing down at the murky waters, willing Grif to show up. The sun was starting to set over the horizon, casting dark shadows to lengthen from the mangrove trees growing from the shallows. Crickets softly chirping, the occasional frog croaking, were the only sounds he could make out.

This was one of the few places he felt safe. Running around these swamps usually calmed him, but not today. Nervously, he fidgeted with his watch again. Grif had said he would be here thirty minutes ago.

After a few moments, he grew restless and started pacing the porch. He heard the trolling motor before he saw or smelled Grif.

Running down the porch stairs, he stalked down

to the small dock. Grif jumped out of the boat and secured it.

"What took you so long?" Kage demanded.

"You are so impatient," Grif muttered. "We have plenty of time. The sun isn't even fully down yet. We would look like idiots showing up this early."

"We need to run a check through again," Kage muttered.

"We've done that dozens of times," Grif said, frustrated. "Is that the shirt you're going to wear?"

"We will do it a dozen more times," Kage growled, ignoring his question. "We can't have one misstep. Everything needs to work perfectly."

Ignoring Kage's words in return, Grif retorted. "I mean, is that really the impression you want to make?" He kept his back turned to Kage.

Kage looked down at his shirt in confusion.

"What's wrong with the shirt?" he said, uncertainly. It was just a plain black shirt.

"Nothing…" Grif said, his eyes twinkling with laughter as he turned around.

Kage growled at Grif, realizing he had been fucking with him.

Grif followed him inside the house. They checked the doors and locks. Started the dehumidifier up. Checked all the camera angles to make sure there were no blind spots. Made sure all doors and window reinforcement held up. Everything was running just as it was supposed to.

They did a run through of everything twice. Kage trying to foresee any problems before they might run into them. Nothing could be allowed to be left to chance. They needed to predict any mistakes before they happened. Made all the contingency plans before they took her.

Kage had run through the plan a dozen times. Still, he did not feel prepared for what was to come.

Chapter Nine

Thess didn't know how, or why, she let Dromie talk her into sneaking out tonight. It was a week until the tourney. If her mom found out, she wouldn't live to participate in the tourney. Which may not be a bad thing, she thought. She was so swamped with training; it was probably a terrible idea to sneak out.

She shook the thought off and finished styling her hair. She put on the earrings Dromie had gotten her as a good luck gift for the tourney. Emerald square princess cut stud earrings. Shaking her head while looking in the compact mirror, she loved how they sparkled like the sun glinting off the ocean at midday. She chose her outfit to match with the earrings. She swirled in her green dress, loving the way the fabric swished around her legs.

Dromie kept telling her she had a surprise. She thought it was the earrings, but Dromie said no, they had just caught her eyes. Dromie was always collecting shiny trinkets and jewelry. Thess wasn't sure if she should be worried or not. She chuckled quietly to herself. An odd sense of foreboding hit her as she glanced towards the night sky, a cloud drifting to cover up the crescent moon.

She quietly opened the window to climb out. Her mom was already fast asleep from a sleeping drought Thess had put in her tea. She should sleep like a baby through the night and, hopefully, Thess was home in time to get some sleep tonight, too.

She stealthily made her way through the sands, heading away from the shore and their village with her shoes in her hands. Sticking to the shadows in case another siren takes a night stroll. Once she made it to the treeline above the sandy beach, it took her a few more minutes to get to the road. Dromie was already there with her car ready to meet her.

"You look beautiful!" Dromie said. "I especially love those earrings! Are you ready for your surprise?"

Dromie giggled, and they made the trek to The Wave. Thess felt the bass before she could see the lights. The music pulsed through her, speeding her heart rate up to match.

Dromie had wanted to meet up with a guy tonight and she said he would bring a friend. And thus, Thess had been dragged out to the club, since Dromie needed a friend to tag along.

Dromie was talking away about her day and their dates for the evening as they were ushered into the club. Dromie kept giving her a secretive glance and a smile. Thess looked up at her friend in bemusement. She wondered what her surprise was going to be. Also, she wondered if she would be able to sneak out of the club early.

Dromie went to the bar and ordered their drinks. Thess sipped the drink slowly. She was a little nervous about drinking tonight.

She had such a full day of training tomorrow; they had intensified her training this week. Last time she had done this, she had been so tired and distracted the whole day. She did not want a repeat or the lecture that would surely follow from her mother.

After a while, the guy that Dromie was waiting for walked up. Behind him was her mystery man. Her eyes met his. She felt the punch to her gut the instant she saw him. The roar of the club went quiet. Her heart was exploding in her chest. Dromie and Grif started talking. She did not hear the words they said.

"Hi, I'm Thessalia, or Thess," she said to him nervously. Unsure how the words could escape from the pressure in her chest.

He stared at her for a moment and then said, "I'm Kage."

When he got close, she smelled the alluring scent of cyprus. His closeness made her feel nervous, the fluttering fairies dancing in her stomach. When the light hit his eyes they reflected red back to her, showing he was a reptile shifter of some kind.

They sat there in silence as Dromie and Grif talked. Grif offered to go get them another drink as he walked to the bar.

Thess kept looking sideways at Kage. She now knew his name. She wanted to say something to him, but couldn't think of anything to say.

Dromie tried to get Kage to talk, but he just sat there and stared at Thess. His gaze mesmerized her. She could not look away from those dark eyes.

Grif walked up and gave them their drinks. She took her drink, taking a small sip. It seemed stronger than the last drink. Her head was spinning and dizziness swamped her. She had been working so hard she had not had much to eat so it seemed the alcohol was going straight to her head. She sat there holding her glass, thinking maybe it was best she not drink.

She heard people raise their voice behind her, then felt someone slam into her back. They spilled her drink as the fight broke out behind her. Kage grabbed her and drug her away from the fight. She could tell by the tension in his jaw that he was angry.

When they got to the bar, he ordered her another drink. Thess looked around to see if Dromie was ok. She found her and Grif talking. She waved at Dromie and she waved back. Bouncers had gone in and broken up the fight. They had separated the shifters. She turned back to look at Kage.

He had a drink extended out to her. She took it.

"Drink up," he said. Slamming his drink back.

She took a big sip of her drink, then another under his watchful gaze. Feeling the hypnotic stare guiding her to throw caution to the wind. She felt herself get lost in those dark eyes all over again. The warm liquid burned, sliding down her throat.

Her head felt like it was spinning out of control. She took a step and stumbled. She felt Kage gently grab her arm.

"I am going to take you outside to get some fresh air," he said, quietly.

She leaned on him and nodded. She felt safe with him.

"Where are we going?" she said, her voice sounded foreign to her own ears.

He laughed softly. "I told you we are going outside for fresh air."

"Oh." she mumbled. She was having trouble focusing.

The lights were flashing and making her head spin

more. She closed her eyes and leaned into him even more. As he guided her through the club. Everything was a blur around her making her head spin more. The voices and music blending together. He pushed the back door open.

"I don't feel well." she said. She felt the warm breeze caress her face when the doors opened. It didn't make the spinning go away, it just grew faster. Her head was spinning out of control. She leaned on him for support, unable to support herself anymore.

"Take one more sip, babe," he said, gently.

She obeyed. A moment later, the world went dark. A green emerald earring hit the ground.

Kage picked her up. He carried her over to the waiting van, gently setting her in the back on blankets. Behind the wheel sat Lorairia. Theireyes met, locked with his surrogate mother's, for a brief second. He saw the fear and worry in her face. He gave her a reassuring smile and closed the van door.

Watching as the van drove off, he stood there a moment. Knowing Lorairia was worried about him, he sighed. The fear of disappointing her over this last mission ate at him. Maybe one day she would understand. He knew she wished he would give up on this mission to get the land back and reunite the clan and just find a peaceful new life.

He dropped the pathway potion bottle the swamp witch had given him. The potion had been designed so to create multi scent trails and throw even the most talented sniffer off the scent.

He was so glad that he bought two slumber potions. He had one, and Grif had another. They were going to play by ear, who gave the slumber potion to her. If they had not gotten the second, the night could have been a bust.

Fucking shifters causing a fight almost wreaked the entire plan, but it worked towards their favor, at least. It had made separating from the group easier in all the chaos without a less chance of the blame pointing towards them for the fight.

He made his way back inside and found a seat at an unoccupied table. Dromie and Grif were still on the dance floor. No one was the wiser of what had happened, from the look of it.

After the song finished its last notes, they made their way over to his table.

"Where is Thess?" Dromie asked, looking around worriedly.

"She said she needed a moment and would be back, then she walked off. I assumed she was going to the bathroom or something, so I grabbed us a table," Kage said as he shrugged nonchalantly. He watched Dromie intently survey the room before she took a seat at the table with a shrug. She believed him, sighing in relief.

"It won't be hard to miss where we are with you two giants sitting at the table," she laughed.

"Would you like another drink while we wait, or are you ready for another dance, sweet bird?" Grif said as he turned towards Dromie and winked at her.

"Why not drinks first? Thess should be back by then," Dromie replied. "Can you get us pink dragon spritzers, please?"

Grif smiled, then stood up to walk to the bar and order them some more drinks.

Kage felt his phone buzz. Pulling it from his pocket, he read the text from Lorairia

'I made it home safe and I am in bed now. Both of you, be careful. I love you, my boys.'

He sighed in relief. So far, this plan was going off without a hitch. He blocked out the fear that something might go wrong.
Texting back to Lorairia.

'Thank you for everything. I know you didn't want to do this and I couldn't have done this without you. I appreciate you more than you'll ever know. You are the closest thing to a mother I have.'

Putting his phone back in his pocket, he rubbed at his temples. Praying the next shoe would not drop.
Grif had returned, setting the drinks on the table. He kept plying Dromie with flirtation and drinks, keeping her mind distracted. That way, she wouldn't realize her friend was missing. They would not deliver the ransom note until tomorrow morning. They didn't want anyone to be searching before then. Give the trail time to grow cold.
He sat back and watched as Grif worked his magic on the sweet, unsuspecting Andromeda. He would never tell him, but thank Cernunnos, the god of the forest, for Grif. Sometimes he actually came in handy. Instead of being the tool he usually was.
It wasn't until the end of the night that Dromie cleared up and asked again about Thess.
"Thess wouldn't leave without saying goodbye to me," she frowned while glancing around the club nervously.

Grif smiled sweetly. "She was probably tired and saw how much fun you were having and didn't want to bother you. You can call her up in the morning, I'm sure. Plus, didn't you say that she has a tourney coming up? I'm sure she has been crazy busy preparing for it."

Dromie nodded, but her eyes continued to search the club.

"You're right, she does. She's been spending her whole life preparing for it, but the last few weeks have been extremely hard on her. Her mother has been pushing her and putting a lot of weight on her shoulders about her expectations. It's why I've been trying to get her to come out any chance that I can get so that she doesn't break." She nibbled at her bottom lip, pulling out her phone and sending another text to her friend asking if she was alright. She stared at her phone for a moment, but no return text came.

Kage watched as Grif continued, trying to reassure Dromie. They both did a lap around the bar with her to see if she was dancing or had found someone at another table to talk to. Coming up with no sign of her, they walked out of the club together to look outside.

Kage and Grif continued to help Dromie searching around for Thess some more outside the club in case she had just stepped out for some fresh air and relief from the crowds and noise.

They continued keeping up the pretense. There were no signs of a struggle. Everyone she talked to said they had not seen her. After a while, she checked the time on her phone and sighed. She half-heartedly agreed with Grif that Thess must have gone home to go to bed. That was probably why she hadn't seen the message.

Chapter Ten

Thess woke up feeling a sense of wrongness
surrounding her. The air felt too dry, her lips were
very parched, her tongue felt like sandpaper. She slowly
cracked her eyes open, staring at the dim room around her
that was no larger than a cellar. She took a deep breath
before pushing herself into a sitting position. Her body
complained about the movement and she momentarily felt
dizzy.

Taking a breath to steady herself. The black spots
in her vision faded away for the moment.

The air smelled stale at first as she took in her
surroundings. Taking a deeper breath and stretching
out her heightened senses, she noticed the air smelled
different towards the stairs in the opposite corner where
the bed she was laying in was.

She walked to the base of the stairs and looked
up, seeing a large, solid metal door. Taking in a deep
breath, she focused, thinking past the scent of the tangy
metallic bars above her. To her surprise, a lazy, warm,

and deep green scent with a thick aquatic undertone met her nostrils. Faint but distinctly, she smelled old, decomposing wood, Spanish moss, evergreen and cypress with watery blue-green notes and an eddy of hothouse flowers and swamp blooms.

Where am I? She wondered silently to herself as she assessed her surroundings. She had never thought her keen siren senses meant to help track prey would ever be useful.

She tried to think about where those scents would come from. They weren't the fresh scents of the ocean breeze she was used to. She was still wearing her green dress from when she went to meet Dromie at the club last night. She tried to remember the exact events of the last night, but her head throbbed trying to remember. Her last memory was of getting into Dromie's car.

Reaching up a hand up to her temple feeling the slight throb. She licked her lips, her tongue scraping across them like sticky sandpaper. Water, that was what she needed. Surrounded by concrete and brick walls, the only entrance or exit of the room was a set of stairs blocked by the metal door at the top. There was a small window high on the wall, but it had bars and was too tiny to escape from. In the room was a small table, chair, and the bed she had woken up on.

There was a sink where she could wet her mouth. She walked over to it and turned the faucet on, but no water came out. She opened the toilet lid, but no water was in there either, a faint musty stale permeating from it, no chance of fresh water.

Trying to reach deep into her magic, sensing out where the surrounding water around her was so that she could draw it towards her, but it felt miles away. She released her hold, the effort of trying to reach even a drop making her dizzy, and black spots danced around the edges of her vision. She lifted her hands again, taking a deep breath, concentrating on finding the moisture in the air and the water from the bayou that she smelt throughout the room to collect it together.

"I wouldn't do that if I were you, wasting your precious strength and water." A deep male voice boomed through what sounded like a speaker and broke her concentration. Another wave of dizziness hit her, and she recoiled. The pounding in her head increased as she raised her hands to cradle her temples.

She looked up and saw the blinking red light of a small security camera in the far corner of the room. Her hands clenched into fists as she turned to face the camera fully, her hazel green eyes darkening as a storm started brewing in them. Her heart's pace was speeding up, but she tried to make an attempt to calm it. By taking deep, calming breaths.

"Where am I?" she demanded. The room started spinning and faded to black. She landed on the floor with a thud.

When she came to, she was back on the bed. The bed was soft. The blanket on top of her was downy. She looked around the room again. This time, the effort made her head hurt a little less.

She thought maybe if she tried her siren song, the water might come to her. She felt so dehydrated. Her tongue and mouth ached from the dryness.

In a whispered parched voice, she started.

Οι δυνάμεις του νερού, οι δυνάμεις του αέρα, αυτή η σειρήνα σε καλεί σε σένα, Το νερό αληθινό μπλε του νερού στέλνει παλιρροϊκό κύμα Όπως θα είναι τόσο mote είναι.

Nothing came to her. Not even a drop of water. She felt overwhelming despair. Had another tribe kidnapped her? Did anyone even know she was missing? Would they think she had run away? Who was the male voice she had heard earlier? Fear welled up inside her. She shuddered at the feeling.

Pushing the thoughts away, she tried to come up with a plan to escape. She walked the perimeter of the room. Looking for flaws or cracks in the walls. Since there was no water, she would have to use her strength and wit to calculate a way to get out.

Her search revealed nothing that could be used to her advantage. She climbed the stairs to test the door.

Male laughter boomed over the speakers. She jumped, almost stumbling down the stairs, grabbing at the railing to catch herself. The solid cast iron door did not budge an inch.

"Don't despair, little siren. You are safe, but certain precautions had to be made. It is not you we want. You are just the means by which we will get it," the voice echoed over the speaker.

"I don't know who you are or what you could possibly want from me," she replied, pursing her lips. Her stomach let out an involuntary growl. She didn't know what time it was or how long she had been out, but the last thing she had to eat was at dinner before going out with Dromie. Her mind flashed to last night, the images fuzzy. Was Dromie alright? Was she looking for her? Had they also kidnapped Dromie? She looked around the room but she didn't see her purse, phone, or shoes.

"Are you hungry?" the voice asked. She couldn't figure out who the voice belonged to. It seemed distorted over the speakers. He must have a voice changing device.

She thought about his question for a second. Maybe she could knock him off balance and run past him when he brings food. She was a fighter and had been training for hand to hand combat since she could walk. Maybe she had a good chance of escaping if she knocked him over.

"Yes," she said, a smile curving on her lips as her voice dripped with sugary sweetness. "Could I, please, also get a glass of water to drink?"

He laughed so loud it hurt her already achy head. Apparently, the headache wasn't fully gone yet.

She climbed up the stairs, hoping he wasn't watching the monitors. She waited till she heard the footsteps on the other side of the door. When the door cracked open, she turned her shoulder to the crack and rushed it.

It was like running into a brick wall when she hit his chest. She bounced back, losing her footing, and she started falling down the stairs. A brawny arm grabbed her wrists and pulled her close before she could fall.

A warm and familiar masculine scent of cypress and musk filled her nose as she once again found herself against his chest. Heat flooded her cheeks and blossomed in her core.

She felt the chuckle next to her cheek as he picked her up and carried her down the stairs. He had a mask over his face, but there was no doubt now that she knew who it was. Trying to discern his features under the mask.

Her heart raced as she pushed her way out of his arms, stumbling back to her feet. She stared at him, completely flustered.

He handed her a peanut butter and jelly sandwich. She stared down at the sandwich, confused.

"Where's the water?" she glared back up at him, all while grabbing the sandwich out of his hands.

"How am I supposed to eat a peanut butter sandwich when my mouth is as dry as sandpaper?" She raised an eyebrow sarcastically, before schooling her features to look more demure at him.

"Little siren," he whispered, reaching out to tap her on the nose then run a finger along her jawbone. "You really think I would fall for that?"

She sat on the bed abruptly, feeling a little dejected. Why would he kidnap her? And why was she craving his touch again? Why did the trail of his fingers feel so warm on her flesh?

The stress of the situation was getting to her. It has to be that. She needed to discover a way to break free. She would play along with him for now until she had an escape plan.

Using all her years of siren training. She took a deep breath, exhaling as her eyes looked up at him. She looked up at him with the most seductive glance she had.

"Why would you take me?" Her hooded hazel green eyes seductively lowered her gaze to his mouth. Waited for a heartbeat, then looked back up at him. "What are you going to do to me?"

He stared at her for a moment before going up the stairs and closing the door behind him.

"Do you think that is going to work?" he muttered.

"I don't know what you mean." She whispered, huskily. She slowly traced her own lip with her tongue. "I

82

just want to know what your plan is."

She saw his eyes darken with lust. Then they went cold and dark before he stormed off.

Kage could still feel her pressed against him still as he left the basement. Her warmth, her skin, her softness. He went to the porch to cool off. The warm breeze made him feel worse.

He was just here to do his job. Exchange her for the amulet, not develop feelings.He felt like such a creep having watched her night and day these last days and it had stirred something in him. He had not thought that stalking her would make him feel this way. Let alone develop thoughts of her.

She had such a strength that drew him. The way her eyes would soften when she thought no was looking. Those striking eyes, those curves, his eyes could not help but be drawn to her.

What was he doing thinking about her that way? Sirens killed their mates after they were done with them. They were cold-blooded, cruel creatures who ripped men's hearts out without a second thought, he reminded himself.

Did he secretly have a death wish? He wondered.

He pulled his shirt off, tossing it aside. His shoes, his socks, his mask, his jeans followed suit. He stood naked in the morning light, walking into the swamp waters. The cool water lapping on his calves, his thighs, then his groin. The cold murky waters helped cool down his thoughts and body.

Once his head had submerged, he made the shift.

His skin grew cold as it changed into scales. His bones breaking and altering made it difficult to breathe. He felt his muscles tear and reshape. Soon, his body settled into his crocodile form.

The water slid off his scales as he swam through the gloomy surface, clearing his mind and freeing himself. He had always shifted when he wanted to find an escape from his reality. Sometimes, just swimming in the swamps was the most tranquil thing he could do.

He swam the murky water's surface. Head cresting the surface of the muddy waters, his eyes and snout peaking out. His angled body hid down in the depths of the dank waters. His tail swished back and forth in the, propelling him forward. Critters swam away in fear, trying to avoid being his next meal. The cool water against his scales helped cool him off.

Letting the air leave his lungs so he could dive down deeper into the gloomy waters. Swimming below in the dank, dark waters, he felt the quiet solitude he had been searching for. Occasionally, a ray of light shone through, lighting up a spot in the dark.

His eyes watched the light play in the shadows. His mind wandered to the future, wandering once this was all done what would come. Once he had family honor back.

Turning, he made the trek back to the cabin, knowing he could not be gone long. Feeling more centered now, he knew he was steeled for whatever she threw at him.

He shifted back as soon as he walked up the shore. His muscles aching from the transition for a moment. Shaking the muddy water off his hide, the water droplets gleaming on his naked tan skin. Highlighting his strong muscular build. Collecting up his clothes, he went inside to shower.

Chapter Eleven

K age stood looking down at her from halfway down the stairs. He had brought lunch for her and had felt more relaxed, at least until his eyes settled on her. Her arms were crossed in front of her chest and her lips were pursed into a frown.

"What am I doing down here?" she grumbled looking up at him as she heard his footsteps creaking on the steps.

He stared down into her eyes and felt a tug in his core, down to his groin. His mask hid his face and eyes from her vision. He tried to speak as few words as possible.

"Your mother has something that I need," he said as he shifted his weight, his voice a huskier note than he had meant for it to be.

"I may not know your name," she laughed. "But I recognize you. I saw you at the bar. Do you think my mom is going to work with a low life shifter like you?"

He looked at her, startled and offended. He didn't think she would remember him. He growled deep in the back of his throat as he pulled the face mask off. No use pretending now. Now, he needed to figure out how to keep their clans from going to war after this. He would need a new plan, and fast.

"What is it you think my mom would exchange me for?" she said.

"The water amulet," he growled, running a hand through his hair.

She laughed sarcastically. Tears pricked at the corner of her eyes as she continued laughing, the effort making her throat feel raw. She knew her mom would choose duty over her. There was no competition.

"You know nothing at all if you think I am worth that much to her. She would let me die before she gave it up. The amulet and the clan come first, even before blood."

He stared at her for a moment. His eyes roving over her face, contemplating if she was telling the truth or not.

"You might as well at least tell me your name." she said.

He frowned and turned away before going upstairs and locking the basement door.

What if she was right? he thought.

No, this had to be another one of her tricks. No one would prize a stupid amulet over their own flesh and blood, would they? But then he thought about the idea that his father carelessly had gambled away their home, their lands, putting him in debt that had taken years to repay. If he knew about his mother's amulet, would he have gambled that away too? Would he have gambled his son's and wife's life away?

Taking a peek at the monitors on the wall, seeing Thess laying back on the bed, he grabbed open the front door and stepped into the doorway looking at the land, and the swamp beyond it.

He had sent the ransom letter about six hours ago to the siren clan. The note explained his terms. That they would release her in exchange for the water amulet. So far, no response in regards to the exchange had been sent to the destination he had specified

Why would her mother not give up the stupid amulet for her daughter? It was just a stupid bobble. Wasn't the blood it would shed worth more than some dumbass trinket?

His fingers toyed with the key around his neck. He turned back inside and went to the safe, pulling out a chest. He had kept the chest shut for an entire week after his mom died before he opened it up to see what she had desperately been wanting to keep safe.

He opened the chest and looked down at the round amber stone. Gold branches surrounded it, criss-crossing around the outside of the stone. Quite simple, but something seemed to glimmer from its depths. He had looked at the amulet so many times, running his fingers across the smooth surface of the amber stone. He had never been able to work out why it was so precious to his mama. She had never mentioned it before the day they left their home.

He bounced the amulet from hand to hand. It had always felt warm to his touch, like there was something he could reach for inside, but it never came to him.

Memories of his mother and how protective she was of the amulet flooded back to him. In the end, it was just an amulet. It had done nothing but collect dust in a box, in a safe. He set it back in the chest. Locked it up and closed the safe. Would he actually let someone he cared about die over a dumb piece of jewelry? He sighed to himself.

No, he wouldn't.

He went and checked the cameras for the site where Talora was to leave response. Still nothing....

Dromie woke up the next morning. She texted Thess. It did not surprise her when she didn't get an answer right away. She clutched at her head in pain. They had a wild ride last night. She normally didn't drink that much, but Grif kept buying her drinks. That had made her lose count of how much she had.

After an hour, she started to worry when Thess still hadn't responded. She decided to go and look in on her. Make sure she made it home safe. She wondered if her mom had caught her sneaking back last night, and that was the problem. She prayed she had not. That was extra drama Thess didn't need right now.

She parked her car and walked the rest of the way to the siren village, waving at a few sirens she knew on the way to Thess and her mother's house. She let herself in with the spare key Thess had made her. Walking inside the house, she called out her name as she made her way to Thess's room. Talora was passing the room when she saw Dromie standing in the middle, staring at the freshly made bed.

"When was the last time you saw Thessalia?" Talora sternly asked as she stared down Dromie, glancing between the undisturbed bed and the unlocked window.

Dromie stuttered for a moment, torn between keeping the secret that they snuck her out and worrying. She bit her lip for a minute, contemplating. Then she decided to tell Talora about the night before. She hoped Thess wouldn't kill her.

"Last night at the club," Dromie started, fear eating

at her. "I convinced Thessie that she needed to celebrate and relax for all the hard work she's been doing and spend some time together. There was a fight and I don't know where she was after that. She has not been responding to my text messages or calls. So, I wanted to check in on her."

"Why?" Talora screamed at her, raking her sharp nails down the frame of the door. "What were the two of you thinking? Thessalia knew she had the tourney to prepare for. She should not have been screwing around. This would never happen if you two weren't fucking off. Get out of here. I do not want to see your face right now."

"But," Dromie stammered, while backing up a step. "What is going on?"

Talora threw a piece of folded paper at Dromie, who barely caught it before it hit her chest.

"This," Talora stated quietly.

Dromie opened up the letter. Her eyes scanned each line. "Someone has captured her and wants the water amulet. Who would do such a thing?" Dromie said.

"It doesn't matter," Talora spat the words out with distaste. "I have too much to do. Leave and don't come back. Don't show your face here in this village again. I have tolerated your presence for years, even though you are not one of us."

"I can help with the exchange," Dromie said, tears pooling in her eyes. She wiped at her cheeks as they began to stream down her face.

"There will be no exchange. Her life is not worth that amulet falling into the wrong hands. You cannot help. You've done enough harm." Talora turned her back.

Dromie kept the letter and walked out. She was Thess's best friend. She would go to the end of the earth to find and free her, even if her own flesh and blood wouldn't.

Reading the letter over and over as she made her way back to her car, she started developing a plan in her mind. She would go to the club to investigate. See what she could find. There had to be some clue about what happened or where she was.

WAlking to her car she tried to focus on what she could do next. How she would help Thess. She drove to the last place she saw Thess.

Dromie walked to the bar, trying to retrace their steps from last night. She thought about enlisting the two males, Grif and Kage, to help her search more since they had also been one of the last people to see her. But first, she decided, she would walk around the club by herself and see what she could find.

She walked through the inside of the bar, trying her hardest to remember every step they took, who they talked to, what they said. Nothing stood out to her. Details of that night were fuzzy beyond the dancing, drinking and talking with Kage and Grif until almost closing, long after Thess was last seen. She felt panic welling up inside her.

She went outside to walk the perimeter of the bar. Other than hundreds of footprints overlapping one another from people entering, and exiting the bar all evening she found nothing. Not even a sign of a struggle.

With tears streaming down her face, she determined to walk everything over again. She took a deep breath, stealing her resolve. Stamping down the panic before it started again. During the second tour of the outside of the bar, she saw a flash of green on the ground. She knew what it was before she got close.

Kneeling down next to the green earring she had gifted Thessie the night before. Reaching, she prepared to touch it, then pulled her hand back. She didn't want to disrupt the evidence as badly as she wanted to hold on to the one piece of her friend that she was able to find. She was trying to come up with a plan, but her thoughts were wheeling around and crashing into one another.

"Andromeda," her uncle Faulkner said from behind her. "What are you doing out here?" He stared at her kneeling on the ground, worry written across his features.

She pointed to the earring before looking up at her uncle.

"Thess was abducted last night while we were here at the club," she sniffled, her voice catching in her throat. "We were just out with some friends to celebrate her upcoming tournament. I thought she had left early because she was tired, but her mother received this ransom note this morning. Coming back here, I was determined to look for clues because Talora refuses to agree to the terms of the ransom or even look for her. I just found an earring I gave her right here on the floor near the back door."

The flood gates opened as she handed her uncle the letter.

Faulkner briefly read the ransom letter before he looked at his right-hand man, Rook. "Go get Nix," he ordered.

He looked back at Dromie. Bending down, he reached out and pulled her into his arms. She felt so fragile, so unlike herself. "I need you to be strong right now. We're going to have questions for you. But I promise I will do everything in my power to find her."

Dromie sniffled, trying her hardest to stop crying, and wiped at the tears rolling down her cheeks.

A moment later, Rook showed up with Nix behind him. She sat there as her uncle explained what had happened.

"Don't you have security cameras back here?" Nix said, stoically. "It would make all our lives easier."

"No magicals are to be filmed on camera. You know the rules," Faulkner said with a huff.

Nix bent down to look at the earring. He looked up at Dromie. She watched his eyes soften when he looked at her. "Did you touch the earring?"

She shook her head no. He nodded back.

She watched as he cast a spell of clarity onto the earring. He sighed deeply when it was done. He picked the earring up and handed it to her.

"I thought we couldn't touch it?" She said, her chest tightening as she clutched the small jewel tightly in her fist. By the look on his face, she knew the answer wasn't the one she was hoping for.

"A spell has been cast to confuse us and send us in multiple directions. Too many directions for us to follow. It would just slow us down. It would be pretty useless to follow them all, but..." he paused, uncertain. "I know who cast the spell to throw us off, and it's not good."

Everyone waited for Nix to finish, but he stood there digging the toe of his sneaker into the sand.

"Well?" Faulkner grumbled, an eyebrow raised at the witch.

"Cassio," Nix said. His eyes wandered to the horizon. "She is the oldest witch I have ever met and one of the most powerful. She lives in the depths of the swamp. I am doubtful she will tell us who she sold the potion to. They have not welcomed her into the coven in years because of breaking rules with humans."

Dromie tried to focus on the little bit of direction they had. "We have to try. It's the only lead we have. I am not going to give up on her. She's a fighter." She would find Thess, and when they found her, she would be alright. Dromie kept repeating that thought to herself as she slipped the earring into her purse.

Chapter Twelve

Thessalia felt restless. She had been down here way too long with nothing to do. All she could do was stare at the walls and get lost in her own thoughts. No tv, no cell phone, no computers. Just these four walls.

Her brain filled with worries about the tournament-Dromie's safety, his eyes, and water. Closing her eyes, she tried to imagine the feel of the sea breeze on her skin.

She paced around the room for what felt like the thousandth time today.

She walked over to the camera and waved frantically at it. "I am thirsty!" she growled, her voice cracking midway.

He chuckled over the speaker in reply, but said nothing else.

She threw her hands up in the air in frustration. She continued pacing the room.

"I am going to go nuts in here!" She said, exaggeratingly. "I want answers. Let me out! I want something to do. Can I get a deck of cards? Anything! I feel like a caged beast. I'm used to the free open air, the endless ocean, and having unlimited WATER! Or did you forget I'm a living, breathing siren? Who needs water to survive?" She picked up the pillow and chucked it at the camera, which bounced harmlessly off.

"I'll see what I can do," Kage laughed back. His laughter boomed over the speaker.

"You find holding women captive funny?" She snapped. "Is this something you do often? Drug and kidnap women? Having issues with the dating life there?"

"No! I do not make a habit of drugging and kidnapping women. My reasons are my own. And my dating life is none of your business," he yelled back.

"Why do you want the amulet so bad, anyway?" She screamed back at him, her pent up energy causing her to lose all patience.

"Again, it's none of your business. Your prissy ass tail wouldn't understand, anyway," he growled into the mike.

"I'm just so tired of being held captive, cooped up in this tiny room without sunshine or water," she said, lowering her tone and trying to sound more calm. She hoped her change of tone would smooth things over.

"Maybe if I had something to keep me busy until you figured out through that thick skull of yours that no one is exchanging me for the amulet. I wouldn't die of boredom before dehydration," she continued louder.

She hadn't meant to lose her temper. She just felt so caged in. His refusal to answer in any way was frustrating her even more. He could at least give her some clue.

Had she pushed him too far? She wondered. She worried and paced some more. If she wanted to escape, she had to learn to control her temper. Maybe try winning him over instead of yelling at him, she thought.

A minute later, the door at the top of the stairs

opened and closed. She sighed as he stomped down the stairs. He held a ratty old deck of cards in his hand.

Maybe if she could keep him down there. Try her best to get intel. She smiled up at him with the sweetest one she could muster. "Play a game with me, please?"

He stared for a moment, then nodded. His dark eyes were almost impossible for her to read. She walked over to the table and sat in the only chair. He pulled the bed over so he could sit on the edge of the mattress.

Now to try to pretend she was like Dromie and draw him out. She could do this. For years, she had been watching how Dromie did it. She would be nice, personable, and keep his attention long enough to win him over so he would free her.

She smiled as he shuffled the cards. They sat quietly for a moment as she thought of her approach. Figuring out questions she could ask that wouldn't get either one of them angry.

"Gin rummy?" Kage asked as he dealt the cards.

"I…" Thess hesitated looking at the cards in front of her. She didn't know any card games but had seen people playing with them at the club. They didn't play card games in their village because there was always something else to do or practice.

"Don't worry if you don't know how to play. The basic rules are that you have to group cards into sets or sequences with at least 3 cards. At the end they add up to points." He replied pulling random cards from the deck and showing her. Thess nodded in understanding and picked up the cards in front of her, flaring them into a fan shape.

"So, how long have you lived here?" She asked, peering at him over the edge of the cards.

She was going to keep the conversation mundane

and lull him into a calm sense. Get to know him.

"My whole life," he drawled, keeping his answers short.

She looked at him, startled. "I have never seen you before that night in the club about a week ago."

She had never seen him in town, either. It was a small community, They would have run into each other at some point, she thought.

He laughed. "Why would a girl like you ever notice a guy like me?" He gazed intently into her eyes.

Her breath caught. Her heart stopped before thudding in her chest. She felt lost in the deep waters of his eyes. "I would have definitely noticed you," she whispered.

"You think you're going to seduce me with those wiles of yours?" His eyes filled with anger. "I am not the type of guy you would ever look at twice."

She blushed. They continued to play cards in silence. Knowing she had to get him talking. She took it all back. How could she have thought she could be like Dromie and have him eating out of her hands in no time? She would have to try again. Regretting that her mom would not let her go to school so she could interact better with others. She only knew what she learned from her tutors about the other species and humans. Most of what they had to say or teach had nothing pleasant to say about them.

On top of that, he was wrong. Thess knew she would have most definitely noticed him. She had noticed him from that very first night in the bar. He was all she could think of since. She even dreamed about those eyes of his. Plus, what did he mean about a girl like her?

She took a calming breath, willing her racing thoughts to slow. She needed to focus. Get him to trust her and feel comfortable around her. She needed to discover a way to escape.

"I didn't get to go into town until I was fourteen years old." She thought maybe if she shared more details about herself, she might incline him to reveal something about himself. "I was never allowed to leave our little village. I never went to the school with other magicals either."

"Going to school with them wasn't that exciting," he grumbled.

"Will you at least tell me your name?" she asked tentatively.

He stared for a moment then said. "Kage."

She hoped he would say more, but he didn't.

She tossed her hand down. "I win!" She smiled a genuine smile. He smiled back. Recalling that Dromie would tell people about her adventures. She thought maybe she could tell him stories. Get him to relax.

He picked up the cards and started shuffling them. He passed them out for a new round.

"I've only been in the swamp once before. We never travel too far from the ocean, from water," she rambled on. "It was always so exciting to go into town and meet the others and see what they were like. When I went to the swamp, it always seemed so... mysterious."

He listened to her intently as she talked. She smiled at him. Her seductive techniques seemed to make him angry, so she switched to trying to be friendly.

He passed the cards out again. She picked up her cards and examined them for a second.

"Dromie took me on an adventure to go meet an old swamp witch," she said, while looking at her cards. "I remember being so scared of meeting her. Especially after all the horror stories Nix told us. Her house was shrouded in moss and vines. We almost didn't see it as we approached. It was eerily beautiful."

She nibbled at her bottom lip in concentration while readjusting the cards in her hands and organizing her thoughts.

"It was a letdown, though, that she just sat on the porch and rocked in her chair," she said, laughing. "The crone barely spoke, maybe two words to us." She kept going on about random stories she had of meeting magicals in town.

"Cassio," he muttered.

"What?" Thess said.

"Her name is Cassio," he said. "She has haunted these swamps for ions."

"Oh," Thess replied, at a loss for a reply but grateful they were having somewhat of a conversation.

As they continued to talk, he opened up a bit more. Mostly one to two words, but she knew she was making progress. He talked about the swamp and some of the creatures he had met in them. She could see the love for his home and people he had. At this pace she wouldn't be free until after the tourney if at all, she laughed bitterly to herself.

He shuffled the cards for a few moments watching the emotions play across her face.

"You hungry?" He asked casually. Before setting the cards down on the table between them.

"Yes, please," she responded.

He set the cards down, then headed up the stairs.

"If," she started, she tried to hide the despair in her eyes. "I promise not to cast a siren song. Can I please get just a little bit of water?"

"We'll see…" He said, as he stared at her and frowned.

She worried she had pushed too hard. Hoping he would bring her even just a small bit of water. She watched as he went up the stairs and closed the door. Sighing, she put the cards back into the box.

Talora stood in front of her clan. She had called a meeting. She still wasn't sure how much to say, but she knew she had to say something. It was her duty, as the clan leader

"I called you all here for a brief meeting," she said, sternly. "I will be the one battling in the tourney instead of Thessalia this year. Many of you may have noticed her absence over the last few days. I received a letter that she is being held ransom, in exchange for the water amulet."

The hush went over the entire clan, then broke like thunder on a stormy night. The volume rose all at once; they started talking over each other. Asking questions, making angry threats, and other cries of fear.

"SILENCE!" Talora yelled, while raising her hand. She waited till the crowd grew quiet before she spoke again. "We will not allow this to happen. We will not give the amulet up. Thessalia is one of ours, but her foolishness got her in this trouble. She would not exchange herself for the amulet. She knows what her duty is. We all know what our duty is. Everyone knows what their duty is, we will continue to honor it. Just as Thessalia would. This is not a discussion. Now, get back on with your duties."

Talora turned and walked away. She walked into her house and closed the door.

As soon as she passed the threshold, she fell to her knees. Her heart was beating too fast, clogging up her throat. She was having trouble breathing. She had not felt this much pain since the death of mother and Oliver.

Clutching at her stomach, she knew she had to stay strong, but it was impossible right now. She would find the bastard who had taken her daughter and show him the wrath of the gods. She couldn't bear to lose another child. Not ever again could she go through that.

Kage rummaged around in the kitchen, trying to figure out what he would make to feed Thess. His original plan hadn't extended to her staying more than a few days before he would exchange her for the amulet.

He didn't know enough about the way of cooking. His job always left him too busy to bother learning more than basic survival meals. Did the siren not eat certain foods? He tried to remember all the meals he had seen her eat. Most of the time, he did not pay enough attention to the food, unfortunately. His kitchen fridge was mostly bare, except for a package of ground beef, a gallon of milk, some steaks, and beers. He grabbed the steaks out, then warmed up the pan on the stove. Protein was good, everyone needed protein. He sauteed the steaks in the iron skillet. Seasoned with salt and pepper. It was the best he had.

Grabbing mismatched plates, he tossed the steaks on them. He debated going back and forth, then decided he would take a chance and give her a sip of water. He threw the cup on the tray with the food. Just a swallow of water in the cup. Hopefully, she honored her word and drank the sip he got her. Or it wasn't enough to do much damage.

He went and looked at the camera's one more time. The drop off point still had nothing. He knew they had been informed that someone had kidnapped her. Grif had spoken to Dromie. They were actively searching for her. Her mother had done nothing so far.

What kind of mom didn't even try to negotiate for her daughter? She hadn't even tried to offer up anything else, no threats, no negotiations, she just did nothing. It confused him to no end. This was her mother, her sisters, her clan, yet they weren't even searching for her.

Grif had gone and spied on the sirens. They were training and carrying on like nothing had happened. Her mother didn't even seem phased that her only daughter was missing and might be in danger.

He would move heaven and earth to protect someone he loved. Why would the mother not even negotiate?

He picked up the tray and started to carry it to the basement.

Maybe it was time to see if Grif can talk Dromie into getting the water amulet.

Chapter Thirteen

Thess sat in the bed, trying to figure out an escape plan. She was on day three of being here. Four more days till the tourney.

She knew she could not overpower Kage. He was so much stronger than her physically. The bars on the only door were solid and the room's only window was too small. There was no access to her water magic here. She would not be able to escape out of here without help. It was so dry in here she could not call for her water magic. Her mouth was constantly parched.

The parched feeling made her feel so dizzy. Never in her life had she been far from a source of water. She felt like a part of her soul was missing. She couldn't even hear the amulet's song.

She wondered what would happen when her mom denied handing the amulet over in exchange. Would he kill her? Would this actually start a war? Or would her mom go on and take care of the clan like she didn't even exist?

Thess felt a pang in her chest, thinking of her mom.

She had always felt the disappointment radiate from her mom towards her. She was never fast enough, strong enough, or even just enough. The feeling that her mom would rather have had anyone else as her daughter always sat in her mind.

Thess got up and paced the room. Chewing on her thumb in frustration.

When she tried to seduce him, he got angry. When she was friendly, he would open up just a bit, then shut down. No thoughts of a good plan to leave here came to her. She wasn't sure what to do.

She could only think to keep trying to win him over. But did she have enough time to do that? Could she even do it in four days?

Kage watched her from the chair, staring at the monitors. He felt like a creep staring at her all the time, but he couldn't take his eyes off her. She fascinated him.

She was nothing like what he had expected. He had caught himself staring at her when they played cards. His eyes were continually drawn to her as if she had cast a spell. Once she stopped the fake flirting, she made him feel at ease.

She was one of the most beautiful women he'd ever seen. Her dark hair would caress her delicate, pale skin. Those hazel green eyes shifting color with her mood. He could see why men died for sirens. He could see himself following those eyes, those legs, that mouth anywhere. Even into the heart of a storm.

Sighing, he leaned his head back. He was going crazy,

it was official; he thought. Rolling his head back and forth, he tried to ease the tension in his neck.

His phone buzzed in his pocket. He pulled it out and glanced at it. It was Azazel.

He groaned and took a deep breath.

"Hello," he answered.

The line was quiet for a moment.

"Well," Azazel drawled. "Where is my amulet?"

Kage sat in silence for a moment. Debating on how to respond. He had hoped this would go smoothly. It had started out as planned, and now nothing was going right.

Talora still had not replied. She wasn't even acting like she was looking for her daughter. She trained and never left the village, from what he heard.

"Well?" Azazel said, his volume raising. A hint of frustration in his voice.

"I have the girl and am negotiating with the mom for the amulet," he lied. At least it was only a half lie…

Kage did have her and he had sent over the ransom.

"Hurry the process up," Azazel's voice lowered. "I grow weary of waiting. Whatever means necessary to get the amulet before the tourney. I mean any means. Time is running out for you to get it and-"

Azazel paused. Kage hated dealing with the dramatic demon.

"My patience with holding onto this land," Azazel drawled. "I could have sold this for a hefty profit or given it as a prize to someone worthy in my ranks. Instead, I kept it for that little boy. A boy whose father abandoned him after losing everything his family owned. I helped you out and gave you a job to earn back all the money he owed me. I've given you years to repair his debt and interest to earn your family's honor and home back. And this is how you repay me?"

Kage put his head in his hand. He was not sure why Azazel thought he had been helping him out. Last he checked, he had been in numerous fights, fist, knife, gun; you name it, in his work for this demon. He had been close to death so many times because of this asshole.

"I am working as fast as I can," Kage said. "I will update you as soon as I have something."

"That will be tomorrow," Azazel said. "Come by the manor at 1pm. If you do not bring me what I want, Kage Mistbright, you will find out how ruthless I can truly be. If you cannot bring the amulet, bring me the girl and I will do it myself. You can bring the little siren here if you cannot handle this on your own and I will take care of it. Then, we can discuss another favor to get back in my good graces."

Azazel hung up the phone.

Kage sighed. The shitshow just kept getting worse. No wonder he was going crazy.He sat there for a moment before he called Grif.

"Hey," Grif answered.

"I need you to watch Thess tomorrow." Kage said. "Plus bring some groceries. Any updates on the search for her?"

"I am going with Dromie to see Cassio today." Grif said. "Nix, the green witch, is accompanying us. He mentions that there is bad blood between Cassio and Clan Elzora."

"Thanks, brother," Kage said. "Cassio guaranteed she would not let our secret out. Plus, maybe seeing you there will encourage her to honorher word. Keep me updated. I will see you tomorrow."

He hung up the phone. Looked back at the monitors. Thesswas still pacing the room.

It was time to cook her dinner. He grabbed ground beef and figured burgers were his best option until tomorrow.

Maybe he should see if she had any food preferences. See if there was something special she wanted.

He fried the burgers up, stacked it between two pieces of white bread and took the food down to the basement.

He knew he probably shouldn't eat dinner with her, but he couldn't stop himself.

She smiled as he came down the stairs.

He set the plate on the table and dragged the bed closer to the table.

She smelled like the lilac dry soap he had put in the bathroom.

She started talking as she ate. "Thank you for the food and water."

"You're welcome. He said. Sitting on the edge of the bed.

Thess started talking, trying once again to win him over. "I remember the first time I met Dromie…"

He listened to her story intently. Her voice was so sensual. He felt it wash over him. He had daydreams of that sensual voice.

She laughed at her own story. Her eyes sparkled and shifted to a more green shade of hazel as she told the story. Her face up as she smiled, dragging his eyes to her lips. Watching the words the memory playing in her mind like it happened yesterday.

He couldn't tear away his gaze from her lips as they moved. The corner of his lips turned up as he couldn't help but return her smile. He knew that she would hate him when she was released, but he still enjoyed the time they had together.

"Nem used to sneak off from practice with me all the time…" She went onto another story.

As he looked into her eyes, a stray hair fell across her face. She tried to blow it out of her face as she ate and told the story. Without thinking, he reached up and brushed her hair out of her face.

He brought his hand back fast. He hadn't meant to do that. "Sorry," he mumbled.

She smiled and laughed. Acting like it was a natural thing for them to do.

He listened for a while as she rambled on. Watching her yawn, he knew it was time to go. Dreading leaving, he looked down at his feet.

"You look tired," he said.

She yawned again, reaching up to cover her mouth. She smiled a lazy smile. Their eyes locked as they both stood up from the table, the room suddenly feeling extremely small.

I am an idiot; he thought as he reached behind him and grabbed the glass he had set down. He handed it to her. It was only a quarter full, barely a few mouthfuls.

She eyed the water sloshing in the bottle as he thrust it towards her. He held his breath, watching her face as she took the bottle from his hands, pried open the lid and sniffed cautiously, watching him from above the edge of her rim.

"It's not poisoned. It's a peace offering." His reply trailed off as he watched her gently take a sip, watched her tongue lazily lick her lips, savoring every drop like it was the sweetest ambrosia. Words were lost to him as a tight, hot feeling grew in his core as he watched her.

A few more sips and the bottle was empty, the plastic crunching under her fingertips as she set it down on the table and looked back at his face.

"Kage I..."

He could feel himself get lost in her eyes. Before she could finish her sentence, he took one step and leaned forward, brushing his lips gently across hers. Her mouth was so soft.

Thinking she would just push him away, but she didn't. He delved in deeper, his tongue toying with hers. He heard a moan deep in her throat as she melted against him, the warm curves of her body fitting into the hard planes of his.

He reached his hand up, gently cupping the back of her head, his fingers tangling in the strands of her dark hair. He tilted her head more so his tongue could delve deeper, dueling with hers. Against his chest he could feel her heartbeat racing with his.

He pulled back looking at her flushed cheeks and swollen lips. Her eyes were dazed as she slowly opened them to meet his stare. Kage was not sure if he could stop himself later if he didn't stop now.

Stepping back he let his hand clench in the soft strands of her hair before he caressed her cheek. He ground his teeth while he tried to tear away his thoughts from her scent and how it made his skin feel hot and prickly. Focusing his thoughts on his end goals of finishing this last mission, he turned and grabbed the empty tray and crumpled plastic bottle before he stormed up the stairs.

Talora stood looking out at the ocean waters. She had received another letter asking her to exchange Thess for

the amulet. She crumbled the letter up and let it drop
into the ocean at her feet. The paper darkened in the
water before the lapping waves dragged it out to sea.

Anguish filled her soul. She knew she had to do what
was right for her clan and what was right for the world.
She could not allow the evil demon back into the world,
but she wanted her daughter by her side.

She closed her eyes and remembered the day Thess
had been born. Thinking she would never have another
child after her first loss, but then Thess came. This tiny
little baby who depended on her to teach her about the
world. She had tried so hard to raise her to be strong and
brave.

She didn't know how she could have gotten caught.
She should have known better, been more careful. If the
tourney was not so close, she could have hunted down
the pieces of shit who did this and make them pay.

She could sense the despair of the other sirens.
Everyone was on edge. The voices of descent whispered
behind doors, asking if she was a good enough leader
since someone had kidnapped her daughter. Plus, what
kind of leader would Thess be if she was so easily taken?

She heard sounds as the other sirens were
commencing to rise for the day. Closing her eyes, she
tried to get a hold of her own emotions and put up a
brave face. Only praying that her daughter was safe and
discover a way to escape.

Thess snuggled in the bed under the thick comforter
she had found folded at the top of the stairs the night

before. It was a weirdly wonderful feeling knowing she didn't have to get up and train. That if she wanted, she could spend the whole day in bed. It angered her, that it took getting kidnapped to get a day off.

On the night before, she reflected. There was no feeling of fear of him. She knew she should, but she didn't. She believed him when he said that he meant her no harm; he just wanted the amulet. He was quiet but his eyes held no malice. There was something cool and calculating in his eyes like he was always trying to plan the next move.

She closed her eyes and thought about the kiss for a moment. She flushed from the warmth of the memory. A ghostly tingle of his fingers bracing the back of her neck and head teasing her.

Reaching up and swiping her fingertips across her lips, the warmth of his lips still lingered on hers. Sighing, she quickly pulled her hand away.

Why did I let him kiss me? He had kidnapped me! But he also had been so kind and gentle at moments too.

She wondered what he thought would happen if her mother actually gave him the amulet. What could he possibly need it for? She doubted most sirens felt the water amulet's call. No one had ever mentioned hearing the song or feeling the pull. She wondered if her mom did. The few times she had dared to ask she just stood there with that stoney glare. When she had asked others, they just gave her a blank stare.

She closed her eyes hoping she would go back to sleep, but no luck. She flung the blanket back.

She saw a change of clothes sitting on the chair. Maybe it's time to have a little fun, she thought. A sly smile crossed over her face.

She wasn't sure if he was watching or not but she

hoped he was. She wasn't even sure what she hoped to gain from this.

Thess looked at the camera and slowly let her green dress fall off her shoulders, sliding down her body to puddle on the floor. Stepping out of the pile of clothes at her feet, she ran her fingers through her hair. She relished in doing this, feeling so powerful. She smiled to herself, only wishing it was the ocean's currents caressing her bare skin instead of the still air of the cellar room.

Once she finished slowly undressing, she walked over to the chair and started putting the floral dress on and panties. Sensually, she smoothed the dress over her curves. The feeling he was watching her every move hit her, so she took her time. She could feel his eyes on her now. She reveled in the feeling, the power it gave her.

Chapter Fourteen

Kage watched her climb out of bed. She looked at the camera. Her smile was filled with mischief as she slowly removed the dress from her shoulders. He watched as it slithered down her body. He could feel a heat radiating from his center and spreading. Her eyes never left the camera. She had no bra on. Her supple breasts raised and fell with each deep breath she took. Her short, dark hair gently kissed the tops of her breasts and her milky skin glistened in the soft morning light that came from the one window. She slid her fingers into the sides of her panties, looking down shyly for a moment, and slid them down. She stood there for a moment, looking back up at the camera. He felt the magical power in that gaze drawing him in. His heart was pounding so hard it felt like it might break free of its cage.

He watched her slowly walk to where he had put a change of clothes on the back of the chair. A pale finger slid across the fabric, feeling it before she picked it up. She slowly slid the clothes down her body, her movements sensual and practiced. She rubbed the fabric, smoothing it over her curves. He watched her hands glide across her body and could picture his own hands doing the same thing.

She was going to be the death of him. He was as hard as a rock.

He went to the sink and splashed his face with cold water, trying to calm his senses. He closed his eyes and took a couple deep breaths, but all he could see was her.

"At least she changed before Grif got here," he muttered to himself.

His head was hanging over the sink. He tried splashing it again but to no avail. It wasn't helping. He hadn't planned for this part at all. He stood up and pushed his hair out of his face.

He could hear the trolling motor coming closer.

"Fuck!" he exclaimed. "Why for the love of Cernunnos is he on time today?" he groaned as he adjusted himself, then walked to the porch.

Grif was already securing the boat. He saw the stern of the boat filled with bags of groceries. At least he had food options for Thess.

He walked over and helped unload the supplies.

"Has Dromie made any headway in her search?" Kage asked.

"None," Grif said. "Cassio would not even talk to them. Turns out they had shunned her years ago and she holds no loyalty to them. Just sat there rocking in her chair, ignoring us all."

"What you're saying is- I could have asked for a better deal?" Kage said, his brows furled up.

Grif laughed and walked up the stairs to the porch. They quietly put the groceries away. Kage made her a peanut butter and jelly sandwich.

"I am going to take this down there to her," Kage spoke. "You should have no reason to go down there. The fewer people she knows are involved in this the better."

Kage stared at Grif's grinning face before shaking his head.

"I mean it," Kage said. "I don't want her to know you are here helping me. Stay out of the basement. We can't afford for her to find out you were in on this as well. If it leads to war, we can say it was all me. You can stay clean of this. Do you hear me?"

Grif nodded and rolled his eyes.

Kage walked to the door, opened it and made sure he could hear the click of the lock sealing before he descended the stairs.

She was pacing the room. Her smile was sensuous as she peered up at him. In this light, her eyes appeared more green than hazel.

He set the tray on the table for her and started to turn, but she quickly blocked his path.

"Card game?" she said, her eyes glowing.

"Not right now," he grumbled. "I'm busy."

"What else is there to do around here then?" Her smile grew even bigger as she looked up at him.

He looked away, trying to tamp down the rush of desire he had for her. What he would do to just throw her on that bed right now…

"I need to run an errand. Someone is here to watch you. Don't give them trouble." He tried to step to the side, but she followed him.

"Where are you going?" she said, biting her lip.

Kage looked down at her and watched her teeth gently scrape across her lip. He wanted to nibble her lip himself, nibble her. He looked up, trying to calm himself and find his focus.

"Out," he mumbled.

"Where is this out?" She asked, peering up at him and nibbling on her bottom lip in concern.

He glared at her.

"Did my mother finally reply?" she whispered, a small flicker of hope mixed with dread in her gaze.

He stared deep into her eyes, not knowing if he should reply or not.

"Well?" she asked more forcefully, her brows creased in worry.

"Do you really want to know the answer to that, little siren?" He sneered, trying his best to build a wall between them before he got in too deep. Nothing could jeopardize this mission, even his own feelings.

He felt his heart crack as he saw a lone tear slide down her cheek. That one tiny tear and all his defenses broke. No matter how hard he wanted to build a wall and separate his mission from his feelings he couldn't stop thinking about her. Reaching out he grabbed her and pulled her into his arms. She didn't sob. She just stood there with gentle tears running down her face.

After a moment, she pulled back. "I told you so," she mumbled quietly, looking at the floor.

He wanted to run his hand down her face and wipe away the tears. He bit back the "I'm sorry" he wanted to whisper, knowing she had every right to deny his apology.

"I knew that this was the way." She pushed away from him and went to sit at the table, facing away from him. She crossed her arms over her chest and Kage could sense that her emotions were warring in her heart and head.

He wished he knew what to say or do. He wanted to

drop all pretenses and make her feel better, but he knew she would not accept it from her kidnapper and he knew he couldn't afford that weakness. He turned on his heel without another word and stormed up the stairs.

Kage got off his motorcycle and threw his helmet on the bike seat. He looked up at Azazel's gaudy estate

White marble columns stood in front of the gleaming white craftsman house. It was two stories high. The columns supported the wrap-around porch. He walked up to the ornate oak door. A scene of demons fighting in the bowels of hell was carved into it.

He knocked and waited for the demon's dour butler to answer.

The door swung open, but instead of the butler, it was Alistair, Azazel's son. He greeted him and then pointed to his father's study.

They walked the white hall until they got to the study. Everything was so white and bland that it hurt Kage's eyes.

Alistair, at least, didn't give him shivers. He was a slightly less cold demon. He must have taken after his mother's side, but he worked for his father so that didn't say much about his morals.

Alistair opened the study door without saying a word. He went and found a chair in the corner whileKage stood at the desk in front of Azazel.

"Sit," Azazel drawled.

A shiver traveled down Kage's spine. To this day he still got the creeps from him. "No, thanks."

It had taken him many years to hide his feelings for

the demon e, but he had. He would not cower down. He always made a point of meeting his gaze directly.

Azazel laced his fingers in front of him on the desk as he faced Kage.

"I see you have the girl, but you aren't bringing me the amulet. Why is that?" he growled, his eyes glowing with a cold anger. It was the first sign of any emotion besides malice and amusement that Kage had ever seen him display.

Kage felt an icy shiver throughout his whole body from that gaze. He crossed his arms over his chest in defense. "I did exactly as you suggested. You said to kidnap the heir to that siren bitch and she would hand over the amulet without a second glance. The mother just doesn't seem to care that we kidnapped her daughter. Plus, you wanted nothing tracked back to you."

"Then you will have to up your game," Azazel said. "Start sending her bits of her daughter if you have to."

Kage's hands clenched into fists, his back stiffening as an inner instinct raged in his head.

Protect. Protect. PROTECT!

He took a deep breath, meeting the demon's stare, leaning towards him.

"What's my one rule, Azazel?" Kage growled. This was his last mission and he would be done with this demon. That moment couldn't come sooner.

Azazel raised an eyebrow. "You do still want your family land back, don't you?"

"Not at the expense of hurting an innocent woman," Kage said.

"She's a siren. How innocent can she be?" Azazel said. His voice went back to its normal cold drawl. All traces of anger vanished as she shrugged and casually leaned back in his chair. "Get the amulet for me now. I am done waiting. Maybe I'll just hand over that property to... Alistair, what's the name of the tribe his clan has been at war with for decades?"

"Sablepaw," Alistair sighed with boredom. He was staring at the ceiling, his face flat with disinterest so we all knew what he was feeling. He slouched in the chair before picking at his nails.

"I am working on another plan," Kage said. He didn't know what that plan was, but he would think of something. He had to and fast.

"Then you better get working on that plan," Azazel scorned. "For time and my patience is running out."

Kage turned and left the room and walked out the front door. He needed a moment to calm down and took the long route home to clear his mind.

Pulling up to the cabin, he heard strange noises within as the noise from his engine quieted. He pulled his motorcycle to the side of the building and looked over his shoulder to ensure the boat was securely tied down.

As he opened the door, he felt Thess slam into him. His face contorted in confusion and shock as he grabbed her and picked her up. He tried to keep her mouth pinned to his chest so she couldn't cast a spell, but he couldn't muffle her voice in time.

He heard two words he didn't understand before he covered her mouth with his hand. He felt a sharp sting of something akin to a blade and realized the swamp water had sliced his arm clean open. He felt the blood drip down his arm and ran to the basement with her, slamming the door closed behind him.

"What the fuck?" he growled in her ear.

"I want to be free!" She screamed.

He set her down and shook her, staring into her eyes. "Then tell me how to get the amulet. You don't understand what's at stake here. Who is at stake!" He panted, willing away the thoughts and scenarios of what Azazel had suggested.

She stood there staring back for a moment. She tried to pull away but he was too strong. He wouldn't let her go until she had answered him.

"There is no way to get it," she yelled, her body humming with rage. But something else was building in her. "I am not even authorized to be alone with the amulet."

He let her go and she stumbled back a few steps before catching herself.

They stood there glaring at each other. Then he turned and went back upstairs, leaving a trail of blood in his wake.

"Grif, what the fuck did your dumbass do?" Kage growled, after slamming and locking the basement door. "I was only gone a few hours. You didn't even have to go down there."

Grif tousled his hair. "She was bored. I just figured I would play some cards with her and that was it."

"She asked you to play cards with her?" Kage whispered. His eyes squinted in anger as he looked at Grif. He felt jealousy grabbing him by the chest. He tried to control the rage but was losing.

"I am sorry," Grif said contritely, clearly confused by the look in Kage's eyes.

"Just leave," Kage said, pointing towards the door.

She had been playing him all along. He had let himself believe her and lost sight of what he was doing. He wouldn't fall for that again.

Thess was upset that her escape plan hadn't worked. When she finally got Grif to open the door after much whining and complaining, she thought she would be home free. She had bum rushed him and ran for the front door, but Kage had come home.

He was extremely upset with her. She heard him stomping upstairs all morning. He hadn't brought her breakfast either. She didn't feel like begging for breakfast, though. She didn't have much of an appetite that morning.

Plus, what did he have to be angry with her over? He had kidnapped her. It was only natural that she would try to escape. Because he was nice, she was just supposed to bow down and accept whatever he did?

She glowered at the camera. He was the bad guy here, not her. So why did she feel a little guilty?

"Ugghhh," she groaned, then flung herself back onto the bed. She stared at the ceiling, at a loss over what to do next. Then she sat up and closed her eyes. She could practice her spells even if she knew they would not work. She needed do something, or she'd go insane.

Around lunch time she heard the door open. Kage came down with food and scowled at her.

"You kidnap me and get mad at me for trying to escape?" she said sarcastically.

He stared at her for a moment and threw the tray on the table. Then turned to walk away.

121

She was not ready to end this argument so soon. She grabbed his arm. The arm she had gashed. She saw that the wound had not closed. She watched as the blood stained the sleeve of his plaid shirt. He shrugged her off and went back up the stairs.

Feeling the guilt grow inside her, she winced. She hadn't meant to hurt him. All she wanted was to be free. She went from the cage her mother had built to the cage he had built. She sighed deeply, feeling deflated.

Chapter Fifteen

Thess paced the small room. The walls felt like they were closing in on her. She had never felt so claustrophobic in her life.

Kage had dropped dinner off without a word, slamming the metal door behind him. Her appetite was gone. He had changed his shirt and she could see the fresh bandage peeking out. She bounced between rage and guilt. He had refused to give her any more water with her meals since her failed escape attempt.

The rage won. She picked up the tray and threw it at the door at the top of the stairs. The food and the plate crashed into the door as soon as he closed it behind him. She watched as the food splattered the entrance and the stairs. The plate shattered into hundreds of pieces. The mess and noise it made when it hit the door pleased her, bringing a smile to her lips.

A moment later, he came barreling back into the room, huffing with anger.

"What the fuck was that for?" He growled.

123

"Let me out of here!" She screamed.

He laughed while his eyes stayed cold and calculating. "Only in exchange for the amulet."

"You know I can't give you the amulet! You are killing me by keeping me down here. I need to feel the ocean! I need to be surrounded by water!" Her rage shone through her eyes.

He turned away from her, bounding back up the steps. She grabbed the box of cards and threw it at his head. It opened up and cards scattered everywhere.

"I am not done with this argument," she screamed, her voice feeling raw from the rage bubbling up inside her.

He slowly turned, his face filled with unchecked fury.

"Maybe I can get my brother over here and you can seduce him again. Just like you tried to seduce me as well," he yelled, his eyes burning with resentment.

He marched down the stairs, stopping inches away from her. Sneering, he said. "You fooled me once, never again, little siren. You are no better than the rest of your ilk."

"I never tried to seduce your brother!" She sputtered, waves of wrath crashing in her heart. How dare he insinuate that about her in addition to insulting her kin?

"Don't lie to me," he growled. He took a step closer, his eyes simmering with heat.

She could see the anger radiating off him. She took a deep breath in, steeling her resolve.

"Did he tell you that? Then he is the one lying. I just asked him to play cards. The fool was easy to shove past. Weak little serpent that he is." She paused, realizing that he had managed to divert her attention from what she was mad about.

She realized she needed to get back on track. He was

so close and she kept getting distracted so she took a small step back. Her calves bumped into the bed.

She watched as his jaw clenched and unclenched.

Kage watched as Thess, stared up at him definitely. Every bit of her body screamed she was ready for a fight. He was willing to comply.

"Ask for anything else, but you won't get the amulet," she said, anger pulsing from her. "They will let me die here before handing it over. I am nothing to my mother or to any of them. They will never exchange the amulet for my life. They will let me rot to death here first."

"I will discover a way to get my hands on that amulet. You don't seem to understand how important it is that I get it. I will stop at nothing to get what I want," he replied, crossing his arms across his chest. His anger warring inside him as he tried to get a leash on it.

"I don't think you understand what I am saying. They will never exchange the amulet for me. Not my mother, not my cousins, no one in the entire clan would risk it for one life! Especially not mine," she screamed. Her breathing came out ragged with fury.

He watched as her chest rose and fell with each infuriated breath.

"What will happen to me?" She pointed a finger at herself, then gestured to the room. "What's your plan when they continue to not care that I am here? Are you going to kill me? Keep me here forever? Will I live like a caged animal until you grow bored with me? What happens after that?"

Her hair was flying wildly as it came loose from her

bun. Every movement caused it to come a bit more undone until it was falling around her shoulders.His eyes were drawn to the movement of the hair as it flew around her.

His eyes locked with hers for a moment. Her scent, salty but warm and fresh like the ocean breeze at midnight, hit his senses. His nostrils flared and his pupils dilated while his brain screamed mine. He had been denying his inner instincts every time he laid his eyes on her, denying the way her voice and scent made his blood run hot.

He hadn't realized his body had closed what little distance was between them. He reached out and grabbed her by the chin and smashed his lips onto hers

"You're an impossible creature," he whispered against her mouth as his other free hand reached up and grabbed her hair. He forced her head to arch back, exposing her pale throat.

He grabbed her ass and pulled her closer to himself. Feeling her resistance slowly melt away.

Thess watched as Kage's eyes went from rage to lust. She was startled when his arm snaked out and grabbed her. His mouth descended onto hers.

She felt her body relax into his touch, her brain filled with nothing but thoughts of him. She got lost in the spell his lips cast. A soft whimper escaped her mouth.

She felt rage fade into lust. She folded her arms around his neck and melted into him. He picked her up and she wrapped her legs around his waist. He laid her on the bed gently. Feeling the weight of him pressed on top of her, she sighed. His mouth left hers, starting to nibble down her neck and down to the tops of her breasts.

He yanked the dress over head in one swift motion. She was naked except for the white panties she wore. He brought his mouth over her nipple, hovering for a moment before he flicked his tongue across it. Then, slowly he drew it into his mouth.

She sucked in air, her breath catching in her throat. Electricity shot through every nerve as he touched her. She wanted all of him, every instinct in her screaming how right his skin felt against hers. She ran her hands over his back, gripping his shirt and tugging it off.

He brought his mouth back to hers, their tongues intertwined. His chest pressed against her. The warmth of his skin on hers spread like fire through her veins.

She could feel the length of him. His hard muscles crushed against her body. She reveled in running her hands up and down him as he ravaged her mouth. She tasted him on her tongue and knew he had created a hunger that would never be satisfied.

She could smell his intoxicating scent. It filled her senses, making her feel fuzzy, like she was drunk.

He stopped for a moment. She opened her eyes as he looked deep into hers. She almost got lost in the enchantment of his gaze, but then he was gone.

He was sliding down her body, touching her, caressing her. He nibbled on her shoulder and then gently bit her nipple before taking it in his mouth and suckingon it. He then gave the same attention to her other nipple.

She thought her heart might explode in her chest. She couldn't fathom how it was staying trapped inside her when it was beating a song she had never heard or felt before.

He moved to her stomach. Gently nipping at the flesh around her navel. He stopped above her panties before grabbing them with his teeth and gently tugging on them. She lifted her hips to assist him in taking them off. Her eyes met his and locked. She watched as he dragged the fabric down her hips using only his mouth. Past her thighs, her knees, and then her feet. Her legs trembled from his touch.

He smiled at her as he started making his way back up her body. He nipped her calf, and bit the backs of her knees before he finally pulled back.

He hovered over her and met her eyes. "This is your last chance."

"Last chance?" she questioned with a gasp. She couldn't focus. All she wanted was his touch, his mouth, his tongue. Her mind was filled with the idea of him consuming her.

"To tell me to stop." He leaned forward and whispered next to her ear, his hot breath caressing as he left a trail of kisses from her lobe to her collarbone and then peered into her eyes again.

She kept his gaze. "Don't stop," she moaned breathlessly as she arched up against him. "Kage."

"You are mine, Thessalia. I cannot get you out of my mind. Your scent, your voice, you plague my every thought. I have been burning for you since I first saw you. I want to feel your tightness pulse around my dick until you can think of nothing else but me."

He slid back down her body, licking her inner thigh. He then dragged his tongue upward until he found her. She groaned as he devoured her. His tongue cast a spell she had never felt before. A song she had never heard.

She felt the pressure building up inside her and her legs trembled. Her hands quivered as she clutched the sheets. She arched her back up and felt the waves hit her until she crested one wave and lay there sweating.

When she could catch a breath, she grabbed him and brought him close to her. She ran her hands down his back till she got to his jeans.

She slid her hands around the front and unsnapped the button, rolling him onto his back.

She stopped for a moment and smiled mischievously. "This is your last chance."

He laughed. The deep, rich sound caused goosebumps to rise on her skin.

She continued sliding the jeans down past his erection. Down his muscular thighs. Then she dragged them off his legs completely. Her eyes watched every inch she exposed of his herculean body.

Thess licked and kissed her way up him, as he had to her. She got to his dick, marveling at the size. She gently placed her hands around its girth, glancing up when he moaned. His eyes closed as pleasure consumed him and she began to slide her hand up and down along its velvety length until a small pearl of liquid appeared at its tip. She licked her lips, looking up at him before sliding her lips over its length. She felt the pull of his eyes as he watched her.

Thess was caught off guard when he growled and rolled her onto her back, pinning her hands above her head and nudging her legs apart with his knee. He positioned himself above her, his length teasing her warm, moist entrance before thrusting into her in one swift, gentle motion. He paused, panting and reining in control to let her adjust to him. His eyes locked with hers.

129

She felt the fullness of him. Her body hummed to the beat and pace he created. She felt the waves building up again. She lifted her head and their mouths crashed together, their tongues thrusting to the beat of the song they were creating.

She felt the wave hit and crash into her, feeling ebbs of bliss travel across her body. He tensed up with the crash and felt his release a moment later.

They lay gasping in each other's arms on the small twin bed. She drew circles on his chest with her fingers, idly caressing him.

She sat up and collected the sweat from his arms and chest, creating a spell with her fingers. Then she used her other hand to remove the bandage. She hesitated for a second, then sang a water spell to heal the wound she had caused. Her voice was gentle and soft. She didn't want him to hurt because of her.

Afterwards, she lay back down, quietly drifting off to sleep cuddled up in his arms.

Chapter Sixteen

Kage's eyes never left Thess' hands as she collected the droplets of his sweat. For a moment, he hesitated as he wondered if she might kill him, but then the droplets shimmered, fainted and moved to hover over the wound on his arm.

She whispered a quiet song; she had such an alluring voice. It caressed his soul, swam through his mind. They were words he didn't understand, a language he had never heard before but he wasn't afraid. The pain vanished in just a split moment. Glancing at his arm, not even a scar was left behind. There was no visible sign he had ever even been wounded.

He saw a sweet gentleness in her, a kindness. It touched his soul. Even after he had kidnapped her, deprived her of water, she still healed him. Guilt racked through his body as his eyes searched hers.

Nothing had ever felt as right as having her wrapped up in his arms. He felt a tug to his very soul at the mere thought or sight of her. His mother often spoke of him finding a mate when he was younger, but he had never dared to dream of ever finding one of his own. Two souls who were destined to complete one another for all eternity. Is this what it feels like? He wasn't sure. He had encounters of lust, but never did he feel so bonded, so protective over someone. Not even Grif, Lorairia, or his own mother.

Could she ever feel this way about him? Would she forgive him if he took the amulet? No, she would not. He was a fool if he thought otherwise.

His thoughts trailed again to the past few weeks. What had he done to deserve such kindness from someone he had done so wrong? The feeling of not deserving her flashed through his mind. His dark eyes surveyed her face looking for answers but none came.

Pulling her closer to his chest, he squeezed her tighter and pushed the thoughts away. It wasn't going to last forever, but he was going to take that moment and relish it for as long as he could. He drifted off to sleep with her in his arms. Her scent filled his nostrils. Her taste coated his tongue.

He woke up the next morning with her still on his arm. He looked at the wound she had healed. He wasn't sure why she had healed him instead of hurting him. He would have deserved the torture.

Brushing the hair out of her face gently, he looked down at her pale skin that shone in the dim light from the small window. She was beautiful. Her heart shaped face, those pink lips. He traced his finger along her jawline and felt himself growing hard just thinking about her mouth and the things it had done last night. He remembered her touch and the way her skin felt pressed against his own.

He brushed his mouth against hers. She snuggled

deeper into his arms. A warm smile spread across his face. He sat there another moment, watching her. Memorizing everything he could, knowing that it would be one of the last times he would hold her like that.

Gently, he pulled his arm out from under her. She rolled over and stayed asleep. Grabbing his jeans, he pulled them on.

Quietly, he climbed the stairs to make breakfast. Scrambled eggs and toast.

He stared at the glasses for a moment. Should I bring her a glass of water or not? Taking a moment to debate, he shook his head then filled the glass up. He hoped he would not regret it.

When he went back downstairs she was sitting up in bed. He watched as the blanket fell and exposed her lush breasts and stared at the gentle rise and fall of her chest as she breathed. The warmth spread through him like a raging fire.

He walked closer to her, his eyes devouring her. "Breakfast in bed?" He asked, smiling.

"Sure," she said, her voice low and seductive. Her eyes met his and he could see the passion burning in her eyes. He wanted to be inside her again. Feel her soft velvetiness pulsing around him.

Climbing on the bed with her, he laid down on his side and rested on his elbow. They ate quietly. Coyly, his hand brushed hers from time to time.

Kage tried to remember the last time he felt so comfortable with someone, but nothing came to mind. He had always stayed focused on getting his land back; he hadn't devoted much time cultivating relationships. Peering through his eyelashes, he watched her.

When she picked up the glass, his heart stopped for a moment, unsure what she would do. She took a sip and set it back down. Relieved, he released his breath he had been holding. It still surprised him that she had not cast a siren spell on him.

"Why?" She asked gently.

"Why, what?" He asked, confused. His mind focused on her breathing and the soft curves.

"Why do you need the amulet?" she whispered.

His heart stopped for a moment. He was not sure what to say, or how to proceed.

How can I tell her the truth? He pondered. He can't because it would make everything worse. Much worse.

His fingers toyed with the blanket. Rolling onto his back, he laid staring up at the ceiling and contemplated what to say. This would be the moment that she would no longer trust him. No matter what he said, the cozziness was going to be over. Overwhelming sadness hit him.

"There is someone," he started. "Who will exchange the amulet for something that was taken from me."

"Who?" she asked.

"I can't tell you more than that," he said sternly.

"Why do they want it?" She scooted away on the bed and crossed her arms across her chest. "And why do they need you to get it? Why not try to get it themselves instead of hiring you? What did they take from you? What do they think will happen once they have it?"

Jumping out of bed, he paced the small space, feeling more caged than ever. He wasn't sure what he should say to her that would make a suitable answer.

"Tell me who is coming after my clan!" She demanded, lowering her voice and pointing at her chest. "I deserve some answers. I deserve to know the truth"

He stared at her quietly. She deserved it, but he

could not tell her more. At first, he kept quiet to protect himself. Now, he was keeping quiet to protect her.

Bouncing out of bed, she smacked his chest with her fist. "Answer me now Kage! One minute you're hot, the next you're cold. You want me to give up something so sacred to myself and my people, but you won't answer any of my questions! I want to trust you, but you don't trust me! You're such an ass!" She stomped her foot then grabbed the closest thing to her, her pillow, and threw it at his head.

He picked up the tray, moving it to the stairs before she could throw it across the room.

At this rate, I'm going to run out of dishes by tomorrow, he thought.

He paused and just looked deep in her eyes. It was best she did not know who wanted the amulet, lest she convince her clan to go to war with the water demon. That was a war she would not win. Already, he regretted telling her as much as he had.

He watched as her eyes went to the water cup that was sitting half empty on the table. Was this when she got her revenge? And what should he do? He didn't want to fight her or hurt her. He probably deserved whatever retaliation she threw at him.

No spell was cast, She just reached over and grabbed the glass, taking another sip of water.

"Why won't you tell me?" her voice lowered to just a whisper. "I deserve to know this. Someone is trying to steal from my clan. If the amulet was stolen, you don't understand the damage it would do. We would be at war with not one but three siren clans. All while fighting an unknown enemy. Do you not understand what this means?"

"The reason that I don't speak is to prevent a

war. A war with a different kind of enemy that would make your siren clans' fight look like child's play." He said. He reached up and brushed her hair out of her face. "If I don't take the amulet, it will be someone else. Someone who will not be as nice. Do you understand? And to be honest, I don't know what he wants with the amulet, just that he wants it and he is holding over my head something I need to get back. I need you to trust me on this. You don't want to know." He regretted it the moment the words left his mouth and wondered if what he spoke was even the truth anymore.

He watched as her facial expression hardened and felt a sharp stab of pain as she drifted away from him. He wished he had more time before her feelings turned towards hatred.

"It is a moot point, there is no way to get the amulet," she mumbled. He watched as the anger left her body and was replaced by defeat. Her eyes no longer met his.

Reaching up, he stroked her check. She swatted his hand away in frustration and laid down on the bed, turning her back towards him.

He waited for a moment, trying to be thankful for the one night they had before she went back to hating him. Then he walked up the stairs, dejected.

Thess laid there for a while. Her chest felt so heavy. She could barely catch her breath. She tried to do her breathing exercises to release the pain, but they weren't working. Hot tears were welling up in her eyes. She buried herself deeper in the blanket.

She wasn't even sure why she thought Kage would

magically open up and trust her. He had kidnapped her; he held her hostage. Why would she expect him to talk to her?

Her feelings raged hot and cold between anger and despair. One minute she wanted to shake him, the next hug him. It was so foreign to her to have such a range of emotions storming through her body.

She touched her mouth, remembering how gently his lips had been on hers that morning. How his eyes held such tenderness as he brought her breakfast. How delicate his hand was when he touched her.

What do I have to do to get him to trust me? She pondered.

Closing her eyes, she took a few breaths, hoping to calm her racing thoughts and heart. Nothing was helping, she felt more anxious than before. She could not stop the thoughts from tumbling through her head.

Maybe that was the problem. She was developing feelings for him. She hated it. The uncertainty she felt had her heart fighting her mind. A war was raging inside her and she didn't know which side she wanted to win. She didn't know what was going on with him. Was he feeling the same? If he did, why did he not tell her what was going on? He must not feel the same. She was just someone who had something he wanted.

Her thoughts wandered on to her family and friends. How was Dromie? What was her mom doing? Was anyone looking for her? Did they even miss her? Were they worried? She wished she could talk to Dromie and Nem and tell them what was going on inside her heart.

Tears started streaming down her face. She curled up in a ball on the bed, throwing the blanket over her head. She tried her best to stay quiet, she could not face him now. She wanted to be alone. Rage melted away and sadness enveloped her until she was crying into the pillow to muffle her sobs.

The tears came down in earnest under the covers until she had no more tears to cry. She just laid there in solemn silence.

Chapter Seventeen

Kage sat and watched Thess through the cameras. When he saw her curl up in the bed crying, it felt like his heart was being ripped from his chest.

Jumping up, he walked to stare out at the swamp. The rising sun glinted through the mangrove trees and reflected off the surface of the murky waters.

What am I supposed to do? He thought. What if I manage to sneak in and take the water amulet, would it start a war with the other siren clans? Put her life even more at danger?

He brushed the hair out of his face, realizing there was no easy way out. He buried his face in his hands, unable to stomach watching her anymore.

She would not betray her people. Her loyalty was courageous and commendable. It made him feel…

He shook his head, trying to get the thought out of his head. What if he overpowered the siren guards? That was too close to the water. He didn't stand a chance against so many of them. His mind wandered back to thoughts of war. She was probably right, it would cause a war with the other siren clans.

Could he put her in danger of fighting in that war? A war that would start because he helped the water demon out? Could he keep her trapped until the war was over? Would she hate him even more than she already did if he did any of those things?

He slammed his fist into the wall and started pacing the room. Why did he care what happened? No one cared what happened to him or his clan. Where were any of the other clans when his mother needed help?

"Fuck 'em all," he muttered.

He stopped pacing when he heard Thess quietly crying from the speakers. He had done this to her. She was crying because of his actions. How could he cause her more pain?

He looked at the safe. What if he gave Azazel his mother's amulet? Would he leave her and her clan alone? Could he betray his mom and break his promise? The amulet was doing him no good locked up in his safe. It was just a trinket that held no value to him. The only value was what his mom had put on it.

His eyes shifted back to the cameras. Thess was curled up in a ball under the blanket.

I will try, he thought, for her.

A wave of emotion hit him as he realized the extent of his feelings for her. He ached knowing she would never return the feelings back to him.

He was in love with her.

He wished they had met under different circumstances. Maybe she could have grown to care about him. Sighing, he knew she could never love a beast like him. Especially after all he had done to her. He had been a fool to think for even a moment she ever could.

It had been settled then. He would offer his mother's amulet in exchange for his homelands, estate, and Thess's freedom. If Azazel accepted the offer, he would set her free knowing she'd be safe to return to her people. She would never have a reason to come back to the swamps. He would make sure to never have a reason to leave.

He felt his heart break in his chest.

He went outside, jumped in the boat, and went to Cassio's house.

The old woman sat on the porch, rocking in her chair. She smiled when their eyes met.

"I need a sleeping drought," he told her softly.

"What are you willing to pay for it?" her gravelly voice rasped.

"I don't know," he muttered, shamefully looking at his feet. He had left with no money, no wallet. "I have nothing on me at this time. I can bring back the money later, whatever amount. Please, I just need the drought."

"How about you owe me a favor?" She asked. He looked into her faded gray eyes. Her long white hair flew wildly around her kind-looking face.

Not many people visited her. Hell, he rarely even visited her. He would have to make sure that changed.

"Anything you want," he said, trying to muster up a small smile.

She nodded, then slowly raised herself up with her cane to get out of the rocking chair. He extended his hand out to her in support. She grasped it, her grip quite strong for the frail old woman she appeared to be.

They walked inside together. He looked around the cottage and saw shelves filled with bottles stretched across two walls. No bottle had a label. He wondered how she could know what was in each one.

. Quietly grabbing various bottles,she poured the contents into a bowl, all the while whispering an incantation.

"You sure this is what you need, boy?" She asked. Her kind old face looked up at him.

He nodded and she patted his hand as she handed him the drought.

Kage made his way back to the cabin. When he got inside, he glanced at the monitors. Thesswas still curled up in the bed.

He made up the tray with food for her. Grabbing a water bottle, he took off the top and poured some down the drain. Then he took the vial of sleeping draught from his pocket and poured the clear liquid into the bottle before replacing the lid. Opening the door to the cellar, he set the tray on the top step, an offering of peace and forgiveness before shutting the door.

Grabbing his phone, he sent Azazel a text message saying they needed to meet up. He hoped this plan worked. He didn't have anything else to offer.

Kage rubbed the amulet one last time in his pocket, wishing he had found another way. Sorrow filled his soul, knowing how upset his mother would be. It was one of the few things he had left of her. He hoped that, had she been alive, she would understand why he was doing what he was.

Azazel pulled up. His white Bentley gleamed in the sunlight. How he kept it so pristine on those dirt roads was a miracle.

The demon was alone for once. He rarely saw

him without his guards and wondered if he could take him down and end it all there and then. Snap his chilly little neck and rip out his black, still beating heart. He knew he would cast a spell before he could get within range, though, so he held back.

Azazel gazed at him intently, trying to hide the rage and despair warring in his soul.

Kage slowly pulled out the amulet, opening his hand up. The pit in his stomach grew bigger as he stared at the amber glowing in his hand.

Azazel sucked in a breath, shock written all over his face.

"I thought it had been lost ages ago," Azazel whispered, reaching out for the amulet.

Kage closed his hand before Azazel could touch it. "I get my land back, our partnership is over and you stay away from the sirens?"

Kage watched the range of emotions cross his face. Shock, confusion, and finally smug joy.

"Done," Azazel said, his face emotionless again. A chill went down Kage's spine.

The knot in his gut grew bigger. This demon had shown him so much emotion in the last minute; he knew that he truly fucked up. Worry sunk in, clenching at his guts. He contemplated running with the amulet but knew he would still go after Thess.

Azazel pulled the deed to the land out and Kage paused.

"Swear it, Azazel," Kage said, after a moment. "I need your guarantee."

"I swear that in exchange for the amulet, I will give you back your rotting family land, I will not set foot on siren territory, and our partnership is over. I have more reliable employees, anyway," the demon drawled, staring at Kage's hand.

Kage looked down at his hand regretting giving the amulet up, but he knew he had no other choice. He had to keep her safe. This was the only option he had so he opened his hand. The demon grabbed the amulet and walked away.

He looked at the deed to his family land laying on the ground where the demon had dropped it. He had spent so much time working and hoping for this moment. It shocked him how little he cared about it now and how cold he felt. It was such a hollow win.

Bending over, he picked it up. No emotion but numbness was in his heart.

The Bently sped off down the dirt road. He stared at the dust trail the car left behind. His heart felt heavy. After the dust had finally settled, she hopped on his bike and headed out.

It was nightfall when he got back to the house. Quietly, he crept down the stairs. Thess was nestled up fast asleep on the bed. Tear trails stained her cheeks. The pain he had caused tore his heart in two.

He bent down and brushed a strand of hair out of her face then slowly leaned in and brushed his lips across hers. She sighed in her sleep. He looked over and saw the tray of half eaten food on the table with the empty water bottle. It should buy him enough time to take her close to her village and head back.

He lifted her up off the bed and let her head fall to rest against his chest. She snuggled deep into his arms, her hand resting over his heart.

He slowly carried her up the stairs and out the front door to where his boat waited in the dark at the water's edge. He gently laid her down on a nest of blankets he had pulled from his bed. Even in her sleep, he wanted her comfortable. He started the boat's motor. It quietly purred to life and he guided them down the saltwater wetlands towards the ocean.

The mangrove trees and bushes were starting to thin out so he pulled the boat over and docked it on the shore with ease. He continued on foot, carrying her wrapped in the blankets. He didn't dare take her all the way to her village, but he wanted her to be safe and protected. There were old caves a few miles down from where she lived. He had found them when he scouted before. He nestled her down in one and wrapped the blankets around her. He pulled his jacket off and covered her up with it too.

He stared at her longingly, memorizing every bit of her. The way her hair fell onto her cheeks, the soft sound of her breathing in her sleep, her lips slightly open. He bent down and lightly kissed her one last time before turning and walking away.

He found a spot in the trees out of sight so he could watch and make sure she stayed safe. He sat there for hours until he saw her run off to her village.

The waxing moon didn't provide much light as he stalked the trails he knew by heart and scent. Kage had only stopped at the cabin long enough to pack his bag with the few belongings. Now he was going to his childhood home for the first time in a while. As he headed to the estate, the sun was beginning to rise and the stars were fading into brightly colored skies.

The front door stood askew. Plants were growing up through the gaps in the wood flooring of the wrap around porch. It looked like the demon had let parties go on in the early years he had held ownership, then let it go to rot. His blood boiled as he looked around at the broken furniture, torn rugs and trash that covered the floor.

He went to work cleaning the place up. He knew he would not be sleeping for a long while, so, he started by clearing a path and pulling the plants off the patio and the walls.

Upon further exploration he found an old broom, bucket, and mop in the pantry. By some miracle, the water in the kitchen sink still worked.

He went outside and found his dad's old ax, rusty with age, on the side of the property. He started taking out his frustration on the dead, fallen trees around him as tears streaked his dirty face. When he finally stopped he was panting with exertion and had chopped enough wood to keep the enormous fireplace in the living room lit for weeks. He loaded his arms and carried it inside before cleaning the cobwebs and started a roaring fire.

The estate was just as large as he remembered it. Over twenty bedrooms, multiple bathrooms, a vast kitchen, library, and ballroom.

He lay himself down on a small mattress and stared at the fire, finally drifting off to sleep only to dream of those hazel green eyes.

Chapter Eighteen

Azazel held the Earth Amulet in his hand. He turned it around and around.

It wasn't the one he had gone for but it was one he also needed. Little did that oaf of a shifter know what he had in his possession all long. Azazel had been trying to swindle it out of his old man for years, but he insisted that he hadn't set eyes on it. He thought it had been lost and would take the powers of the other amulets to draw it out of darkness.

He smiled ruthlessly to himself as he ran a thumb over the cold stone of the amulet. He would have to make his own plan to take the water amulet from the sirens eventually, but that could wait. As long as someone else went on their land, he wouldn't be breaking his word. His son, Alistair, could be the one put in charge of taking the water amulet. The fool of a shifter hadn't even asked that his men not set foot on the land.

Let them think they were safe while he plotted and worked to collect the other amulets. He had time on his side. He would go after the other amulets first, then come for them.

He looked at his son sitting across his office. Alistair was half water demon and half fae. His ashen blonde hair showed hints of fire red highlights as he shifted in his chair. He had the pale skin of the fae, a few shades darker than his dad's. His gray-blue eyes shone with boredom. His ears were demi-pointed, a trait he had gotten from his mom. He grimaced at his father's behavior. His ever so slightly elongated canines, another trait of the fae, glinted in the light of the room.

"Alistair, let's celebrate. We are one step closer to achieving our goals and taking over this pathetic region of the world. Imagine that shifter's surprise if he ever learns what a prize he traded me for that shithole of a place he calls home." He grinned, tossing the amulet into the air and catching it before tucking it into his pocket.

Alistair turned to look over at his father from where he was sitting staring at the moonless night sky.

"But what of the girl and the sirens? Now that they know someone is after their amulet, their guard will be higher than ever.." He grimaced, changing his position in the chair and crossing his legs to meet his father's stare.

"We will take care of that later. Give them time to let their guards down. Plus, when we come to get it with the other six amulets in hand, our powers will easily outweigh theirs."

"Who do we go after next?" His son inquired, tugging at the cuffs of his sleeves.

"That is the question, isn't it? The water birds will be too obvious. Their princess…" He emphasized the word, "is best friends with that siren bitch. They'll have heard of the threats to exchange it and be more cautious. No, we must think of who would be least suspicious of the siren's tales of woe."

Once Azazel had all seven amulets, he could wake up Calpa the Kelpie Demon, the first of her kind. The most powerful of her kind. Once he possessed her, his power would make even the hurricanes of the region look like child's play.

Chapter Nineteen

Thess could hear the hushed rhythmic sounds of the ocean lapping against the shore. She felt disoriented at first.

A lone cry from a sea bird echoed in her ears. She must be in a dream, she thought as she took a deep breath, her nose filling with his scent. Her heart warmed and skipped a beat at the memory of falling asleep in his arms on that tiny bed, just the two of them without a worry in the world. Then, reality hit her like a tsunami. A twist of life's cruelty for it threw them both into this tragic situation. She wished they had met under different circumstances.

She wanted to apologize for her behavior and words when she last spoke with Kage and decided to get up to do just that. She stretched out, feeling her toes dig deep in to the sand.

Sand? She sat up quickly, opening her eyes and throwing the heavy blanket off her chest. No, it wasn't a blanket. It was his jacket, and she wasn't in that little room anymore. She crouched down on her legs, ready to spring at the first sign of danger as she looked at the surrounding area. She was deep in a cave, alone. The smell of the ocean drifted in with the dim light from the night sky at the entrance.

"Kage?" She whispered quietly while getting to her feet and wrapping his jacket around her shoulders. Her only answer was her own echo, bouncing back to her.

The cave was dark, dim light shining through crevasses in the rocks. She walked to the entrance. She looked out to see the darkness of a moonless night. The smell of the sea wafted toward her. She felt a sense of peace wash over her as she heard the familiar song of the waves. The water amulet was close. She looked to the east and could see the spark of flames touching the sky as the sun was beginning to rise.

The familiar landmark of the cliffs that guarded the back of her clan's land lay a few miles to the north.

Why am I in this cave? Where is Kage? What about the deal? What did he do, that foolish shifter? Is he hurt? She thought.

Rage and despair filled her gut at the thought of him. He said that boss of his wanted nothing except the water amulet. Was he foolish enough to set her free and try to steal it for himself?

She steeled her resolve and started running north across the beach towards her village. She prayed she was not too late. That he had not tried to fight her clan to get the amulet.

She ran to the temple. The guards jumped in surprise to see her as she rushed past them through the door. She stared at the amulet sitting on its pedestal in confusion.

He hasn't tried to steal it, She thought to herself as the guards came to stand around her.

They blocked her from leaving the temple. She

barely heard their questions, but she heard Talora's name somewhere in the mix. She continued to stare into the blue depth of the diamond on the amulet, watching it pulse in the same rhythm as her conflicted heart.

Her mind filled with the lullaby of the water amulet. He was not here and there were no signs of a battle in the temple.

When she saw Kage again, he better be ready because she had a lot she wanted to say to him.

Thess had one day left. Talora wouldn't even let her sleep alone anymore. Her mom was by her side day and night.

The thing that caught her off guard the most was when her mom had run into the temple. Thesshad seen worry and fear in her eyes. All her life, she had thought her mom didn't truly care for her, but maybe she had been wrong. Tonight was the ceremony asking for the blessing of the sea goddess Amphitrite.

She had to do a cleansing ritual first, bathing her in blessed waters. Then they put the oils on her skin. The sirens prepared her by dressing her in ceremonial garb. They had draped the light golden toga around her body.

She was tired of being touched by the other sirens. All she wanted was to be alone. Every second of the day since she returned she had someone there. Her mind drifted back to Kage. There was not one attempt to take the water amulet or to talk to her. Her mind drifted, wondering if he was alright.

Confusion and sadness flowed through her, ebbing and flowing. She wanted to go out to find him and find out why, but her mom would not let her out of her sight. She had not even received a chance to explain to Dromie what had happened.

The story she told them was that she had no clue who kidnapped her, but she had escaped. She had gotten lost and turned around, so could not tell them where they had held her hostage. The words had escaped her mouth before she even had time to think. She could not tell them Kage was involved.

Dromie walked into the room on cue like she could read her thoughts. She smiled at her, trying to hide the ache and sadness. She knew by the look in Dromie's eyes that she had failed.

Bouncing up, Dromie smiled back. "You look and smell beautiful!"

"Thank you," Thess said demurely.

"Thess," Dromie whispered. "Will you tell me what's going on with you?"

Thess looked at her, but knew too many ears were around. She just smiled half-heartedly.

Talora entered the room.

Thess looked at Dromie and shook her head.

"It's time," Talora said. Her voice had been less harsh lately. She reached up and adjusted her hair gently.

The attending sirens opened the door for her. Her sandals crunched on the sand as she walked the same path she had trekked millions of times. The waxing moon in the sky lit the path. Pulling her shoulders back and her head up, she watched as the temple stood before her.

Sirens stood on each side of the building. Dromie stood by the entrance; she winked at Thess. Asiris, the priestess, stood behind the amulet. Her daughter Nem stood to her right.

Thess let the song wash over her, finding a bit of peace. The magic of the amulet pulled her eyes to it. She watched as the flames hidden in its depths shined.

Asiris started the chant to call for the blessing on her.

Amphitrite, goddess of the sea, powers of water, powers of air, these sirens call to thee. Moon above and sea below, ancestors ancient and old, spirits from beyond the misty veil of silver, safeguard our guardian, our champion, Thessalia Potamides.

Blood to blood and heart to life let this new cycle begin and our new champion be blessed by you, mighty Amphitrite.

She heard the sirens behind whisper in unison. "Blessings Amphitrite."

Thess bowed her head so she could put the amulet on her. Looking down,she marveled at its beauty and then closed her eyes. She felt the flow of magic wash through her veins. She no longer was filled with fear at the magic she felt from the amulet. She reveled in the feeling and stood for a moment.

The cheering jarred her out of her reverie. Her smile was tentative as she looked around at everyone.

Her focus had been off these last days, her mind constantly wondering about Kage. Was he alright? Why had he released her? Why had he not come to see her? How could she get back to the cabin to find him?

Sighing deeply, she returned to the present. The ship that would take them all to the island for the tourney stood in front of them.

A magical mist had been called to hide their journey. Two sirens sat at the helm of the ship, singing the spell of mist. As per ceremony, she would be the last to get on the ship.

The ship was hundreds of years old. The wood was stained dark and worn. It was the same ship that had brought their clan over from their homelands when the war happened.

Its pale white sails stood out against the night sky. She looked at all the faces staring down at her with such hope. After all the sirens and Dromie were on board, she walked the gangplank. The sway of the boat was hypnotic, the mists surrounding it made it feel like she was floating in a dream.

The waxing moon guided their path to the island. She glanced around seeing other ships were arriving as they were.

A magical barrier that only few could see through surrounded the Cyrene island. It was a lush tropical land filled with magical animals found nowhere else on earth. A small herd of unicorns ran the length of the beach. Pelts of black, brown, and white raced across the sands. The white plumes of the caladrius bird shone in the moonlit sky.

As she disembarked, the earthy smell of the jungle hit her. She had never been here before. She surveyed the land, trying to absorb all its beauty. There were five paths and five docks, each marked with a clan's name. One clan was long gone, only four ships docked. One dock and one path stood empty of sirens.

They stepped onto their path and walked through the jungle on a trail that was well worn. Two sirens in front of her carried a torch to light the way. It was almost pitch black under the canopy of the trees.

The white travertine limestone columns of the colosseum shone in the firelight as they approached. Torches stood at the entrance that held their clan name spelled in their home language above the doorway. The main doors stood open already and lead into a grand hall.

This is where they would stay and prepare for tomorrow night's fight. Pacing the room, she surveyed it. rescos of siren battles of the past were interspersed on the white walls.

She paused when she saw one of her mom. Staring intently, she was not sure which battle it was. Talora looked beautiful in the painting. Her dark hair was flying behind her as she wielded a sword above another siren's head and water swirled around them.

"Soon you will grace these walls," Talora stated, sounding so matter of fact.

Thess looked at her mom. She had never thought her mom had faith in her until these last days. "You think?" The lack of confidence shone in her tone.

Talora met her gaze. "Yes."

Thess felt tears swell in her eyes as she reached for her mom and hugged her. They stood there for a moment locked in an embrace. Her mother had rarely shown her physical affection before, but she'd hugged her several times that week.

A figure in a white robe walked into the room. Talora went down on her knees, bowing her head and motioning for Thessalia to do the same. Behind them, she could hear the rustle of clothes and scraping on stone as the rest of their clan followed suit. A rich voice filled the chamber and echoed off the walls. The voice was ancient but also young and she could feel its strength to the core of her bones.

"It is time, Thalassic," the voice said as the robed figure raised a pale white hand, palm up.

Talora nodded, then reached towards her daughter, lifting the amulet from her neck and placing it in the hand.

The moment the amulet left her body, Thess felt its weight and warmth leave her, causing goosebumps to rise on her flesh and a chill to run down her spine.

'Do not fear, child. Prove your worth and shine bright as the northern star,' A gentle voice spoke in her head.

She looked up to see the soft pink lips under the hood quirk into a smile before turning away and heading down the dark hall.

Thess lifted a hand to where the amulet had hung and rubbed at the spot on her chest.

The room filled again with quiet chatter as everyone moved to stand and continue looking around the room. After a moment, everyone started to pull up a mat and go to sleep.

Thess found Dromie waiting patiently in the back and nodded to a corner that was empty. They both met away from the others..

"What's up?" Dromie asked. The worry in her eyes was still there, even after all these days.

"I just wanted to sit here and listen to you tell me all the gossip I missed," Thess said, chickening out from telling the truth. If she said what had happened, she knew she would break down. With so many eyes watching, she could not afford that.

They both lay on mats as Dromie talked about all the magical creatures in town. It was relaxing to hear the stories and step away from her own life, even if it was just for a brief moment.

Chapter Twenty

Day one of the siren tournament.

The tournament was held on Cyrene islands close to the Bermuda Triangle. A magical mist protected the island from view and discovery for as long as their history recorded. The mist would befuddle sailors who crossed near, causing them to lose sense of direction and change course.

On the island stood a massive limestone coliseum surrounded by benches and alcoves. The gleaming white walls contrasted against the lush green of the jungle surrounding it. Creatures and clans came from around the world once every 25 years to watch the tournament.

For hundreds of generations, the five siren clans would compete in matches of strength, magic, and will to win the rights to protect the Amulet of Water and be blessed by Amphitrite. 500 years ago, Clan Aerwyna went extinct and was never heard of again. No one knew what had happened, they just never showed up for the tourney. When the leaders of the other siren clans went to investigate, their island stood empty. No houses, no signs of war, no sirens, just a barren island.

Their antechambers and alcoves were left preserved and undisturbed in memory as the four remaining clans continued the tradition.

The surrounding islands remained a sanctuary to the mythical and nearly-extinct creatures of the world. The priestesses and their assistants kept watch over the islands and protected the traditions.

The gates were opened at sunrise as all the clans gathered before them. They cast a spell to illuminate all five of the entrances. Three priestesses in hooded white robes stood on the embankment of the coliseum wall. Between them, displayed on a pedestal, was the Amulet of Water. Its gemstone shone in the soft sunlight as the sun crested the colosseum walls.

A dwarf came out of the entrance to greet them and lead them to a feasting hall. Each clan had a table set for them. Food and drinks were overflowing to celebrate another chance at victory and to honor the Goddess.

Thess looked towards the north wall and saw their clan names carved in the relief in the limestone leading to the alcoves that surrounded the coliseum. She glanced down the wall. Each gateway had the name of a clan. Only one entrance stood barren as no one was there to join in the festivities.

Thess steeled herself for the tourney. Soon, they would announce who was going against who on the first day. Two battles to be had, four clans fighting.

The coliseum was crowded with a mix of spectators and each of the clans. The coliseum floor was flooded with about a foot of water. Each corner had a siren clan champion standing alone. Weapons at the ready.

Clan Thalassic occupied the northwest corner and Thess stood in the alcove waiting to hear who she would be fighting.

The herald of the tourney went to the center of the water pit. He was a small, robust troll. One of guardians of the island and its creatures.

His voice boomed through the coliseum "Our first champions to fight are…" he dramatically paused. "Leucosia of clan Poratore fighting Clythia of clan Seyeruhn. Sirens take your marks."

He ran off the floor as fast as his little legs could carry him.

Thess felt relieved and apprehensive that she had a little more time before she had to fight. She held her breath and gripped the railing; her knuckles turning white as she watched the sirens take their places.

Leucosia was a tiny blonde-haired siren. Her blue eyes sparkled with anticipation. In her hand, she held a magical hammer. The markings of spells on it were too hard to discern from where Thess stood.

Clythia was a tall brunette with eyes the color of muddy water. She paced back and forth on her marker tossing her broadsword from one hand to the other.

Talora leaned over and whispered to her that Clythia was new to the tourney, just as she was. Leucosia was going on her third tourney. Talora had fought her two other times and had said that she was a fierce competitor not to be taken lightly.

The horn blared through the stadium announcing the fight was about to begin.

Clythia was the first off the punch to cast her siren song, sending a tidal wave at Leucosia. Leucosia was nearly knocked over, but she caught herself at the last second and cast a water eyewall spell to block the next tidal wave that Clythia sent crashing at her and jumped out while it still swirled behind her. She shifted and the storm went crashing towards Clythia, knocking her to her knees.

Leucosia's eyes showed how much she enjoyed the battle, laughter shining through them. She drug her hammer through the waters by her feet creating a whirlpool. It kept growing and growing.

Clythia finally managed to get back on her feet. Her voice sounded hoarse as she cast her next spell for a cyclone.

The whirlpool grabbed her before she could get the spell finished. Leucosia pounced, bringing her hammer down at Clythia's head. Clythia shifted left, the hammer grazing against her temple.

Clythia looked dazed as she tried to regain her balance her eyes dazed from the blow. She kept shifting to avoid more swings of the powerful hammer. Clythia reached a hand out to bring forth a shield of water in front of her.

Leucosia laughed, sending chills down Thess's spine. Her smile was full of pure malice.

"You think a feeble shield of water is going to protect you from me," she yelled, her voice reverberating through the stadium. "Admit defeat or die. I don't care which one."

Clythia regained her feet, trying to switch the offensive. Clythia swung her sword but was easily deflected by the hammer. She pulled back, trying to gain some perspective, but it was too late. Leucosia brought the hammer down, breaking Clythia's sword arm. She screamed in pain and dropped the sword into the swirling waters and fell to her knees, hanging her head as she cradled her arm to her chest.

Leucosia raised her hammer over her head to bring forth another blow, but the horn cried out to signal the end of the match. Her eyes filled with disappointment as she held it above her for a moment then dropped it to the ground.

The troll came back out. "The winner of this match is Leucosia of Clan Poratore. You shall move on to round two tomorrow."

Leucosia lifted her hammer in the air, turning in a circle to look at all the sirens. Her gaze stopped when she met Thess. A grin appeared on her lips filled with nothing but pure hatred. The crowd chanted her name and cheered as she made her way off the field towards her clan.

Talora turned towards her daughter.

"Now, I hope you realize why I pushed you so hard," Talora stated, sternly. "This is a serious trial that will push you to your limits and test everything we have taught you. You need to be not only strong and brave, but ruthless, cunning, and sharp witted. Delora has been doing the tourney for her clan for the last ten events. She never gets past the first round. That does not make her a weak opponent by any means. It just means she has more to lose if she does not win."

Her mom turned and strode out of the alcove back to their gathering room.

The intermission had started. Thess had an hour before they would announce her match. The nerves were eating at her.

Dromie, sensing her distress, came up and rubbed her shoulders for a moment.

"Don't let what your mom said get under your skin," Dromie said. "You will win with your own magic that you create. You are one of the most powerful sirens ever. I have faith in you and your abilities."

Thess grabbed Dromie and hugged her. She could not ask for a better and more supportive friend.

She turned back to the arena floor. They were parading magical endangered animals around. A griffin flew above them gracefully. Brown feathers glimmered and reflected in the waters below.

"Why don't we get a bite to eat?" Dromie said. "Then we can test your armor fit one last time."

She followed Dromie back to the room. A table was set up with a different array of meats, cheeses, and exotic fruits.

She took the plate of food Dromie handed her and nibbled on various things but didn't taste anything. Her mind was much too preoccupied with the match ahead.

Nem walked up and joined in the conversation. Thess let them talk, occasionally nodding.

The three of them made their way back to the alcove. Thess closed her eyes trying to mentally prepare for the battle ahead. The food was sitting heavy in her stomach as she listened to the spells splashing through her mind.

She walked over to where her armor was laid out on

the table. She ran a hand across the smooth leather chest piece that had been hand tooled with spells of old. Some that had been lost to time. Her mother and grandmother before had both fought with this armor. She smoothed the folds of her toga before pulling the piece over her head. The worn leather fit against her body like a second skin. She buckled the matching arm braces, but her feet were left bare to feel the vibrations of the water. Lastly, she picked up her sword and put it in the scabbard, pacing restlessly around the alcove. Her mind returned to Kage. She wondered what he was doing and if he had thought about her since they parted. She shook the thoughts away; she couldn't let anything distract her now.

Dromie came out to join her. In her hand, she held a small silver comb shaped like a water bird.

"For good luck," Dromie said, smiling. Thess turned around. Dromie brushed her hair, then secured it behind her head to keep it out of her face."

"Thank you, Dromie. I love it," Thess said, feigning a smile.

"It is so pretty, Dromie." Nem stood behind Dromie, smiling. "I didn't bring you anything but some words. I wish you luck."

Thess smiled at Nem. "Thank you."

The troll stood in the center of the arena.

"It is now time for our next match. We have Thessalia from Clan Thalassic fighting against Delora of Clan Aperantos. Sirens take your marks."

Thess walked to her mark. She felt the pulse of the water on her feet. Felt its rhythm beating slowly and creeping up to her chest. Her mother had always said all waters had their own song. She taught her to take a moment and listen to it and that it would strengthen her spells.

Slowly, she opened her eyes, meeting Delora's sea green gaze. Her strawberry blonde hair drifted around her shoulders. Her weapon of choice was a longsword. She stood calm.

Thess heard the horn blare. She felt her song rising up in her but Delora was fast. She shifted her song and threw a massive wave up to block the small hurricane she'd thrown at her.

Changing tactics and spells, she called for an ice storm. She flung it at Delora. She grunted as the ice crystals crashed into her, throwing her back a couple steps.

Thess could hear Delora casting her next spell. She knew there was no time to waste. She cast a solid ice wall to block the assault.

Delora's Cyclone crashed into the ice wall, spraying her with water.

She began to call forth a hurricane. She felt it surround her. The rage and the sadness of the last weeks made her voice stronger and stronger. She felt the waters swell as she stood in the center of the storm. No sounds reached her, just the beat of the water. Her tempo picked up and she felt her feet leave the ground as she reached for every drop of water in the stadium she could grasp. She focused her energy and sent out blasting at Delora.

Delora fell to the ground in shock. Her breath became heavy.

Thess then heard the song, a song she had heard her whole life. The amulet's song was reaching out to her, giving her confidence. She jumped at Delora, swinging her sword down.

Her arm shook from the reverberation when the swords clashed. Delora tried to gain her feet but could not due to Thess relentless drive. She kept swinging the sword over and over.

Thess pulled back her arm to swing again but Delora was a fraction of a second faster. She tried to dodge the blow coming straight for her chest. Delora's sword tip caught in the flesh of her shoulder and sliced clear down to her forearm. Red blood welled up in the wound on her left arm.

A flash of triumph crossed Delora's face as she took in the injury she had bestowed. In her few seconds of delay, Thess pulled back and kicked her square in the chest, knocking her down on her back again. She sucked in a breath as the wound in her arm began to throb and black spots danced along her vision. She was losing blood fast, she needed to finish this quickly before she lost consciousness.

Thess paused for a second to take a steadying breath. The loss of blood making her head spin. She felt a warmth fall over her body like a cloak while a new spell sang softly in her mind. The words crashed in her mind like waves hitting the shore. Sounding so familiar but knowing she had never heard them before. She looked at Delora and sang out the spell. Softly at first the spell came out, then with louder and with more confidence. Thess could see the rise in fluid as the spell called forth to the water in Delora's veins. She felt the water pulling towards her. Saw it manifest on Delora's skin as it collected droplets.

Delora screamed in pain as the water, her life's blood, started to leak from her pores, floating around her body like a hazy mist. "I give," she yelled as her body contorted from the agony.

Thess stopped, stunned, her eyes opening in shock and fear of her own actions. She did not know where that spell had come from or how she could have used it. She backed away, looking across the coliseum to see the others' reactions, but no one seemed to notice what she had done.

The troll ran up, lifting her good arm in the air as high as he could.

"The winner of this match is Thessalia of the Thalassic clan."

The crowd's cheers felt deafening. A bit of exhilaration shot through her. She looked up, catching sight of her hand raised up, sword flashing in the light.

She searched the crowd and wondered if he had come to see her, but she could not feel him or see him.

She was scooped into a bear hug as Dromie entered the arena. "I knew you could do it!" She screamed.

Thess felt the pain in her arm as the hug jarred her.

Day one was over. Thess looked around. She knew tomorrow's battle would be the genuine test of her powers.

Chapter Twenty-One

Day two of the siren tournament.

Two hours before the tourney was about to begin, Thess stood in the corner of their alcove scanning the faces in the crowd. She had come here to look several times. A wave of disappointment hit her again, her heart feeling heavy in her chest when she did not see his face in the crowd.

She didn't know why she even bothered looking. She must be losing her mind.

What did I expect? She wondered. That the man who had kidnapped me to get a sacred amulet could fall in love with me? Follow me to the tourney and profess his love?

She just couldn't understand why he had released her without a word. He hadn't even made one attempt to get the amulet either. Confusion settled in her heart. Then worry. What if something had happened to him?

Chewing her lip nervously she searched the crowd for

the dozenth time. Still nothing. She knew he would not be coming. Even if he had come, would she be able to find him in the sea of people? There were hundreds of faces out there.

Sighing, she turned and saw Dromie watching her from across the room. When their gazes met, Thess's eyes glistened as they welled up with unshed tears, her throat feeling tight.

"Thessie, what's wrong?" her friend whispered, as she rushed to her side.

Concern was written all over her face. Gently she grabbed Thess's right shoulder, turning her towards the wall and hiding her from prying eyes. She reached up and brushed away her tears.

"What is going on?" Dromie asked.

"Kage," Thess managed to rasp out before gasping for breath and closing her eyes.

She took another breath, steadying herself before telling her friend the truth of what had transpired during her abduction and her true feelings towards the shifter. He'd shaken her world.

"Oh, Thessie," Dromie said worriedly while giving her friend a soft hug. "Why didn't you tell me earlier?"

"I didn't know how you'd react." She took a pause for breath. "I wasn't even sure I knew exactly how I felt about it all. A part of me has been empty since he left me alone on the beach after releasing me. Maybe he's made some sort of terrible mistake and he's in trouble. I'm worried about him. I know someone forced him to abduct me in order to steal the Amulet of Water. The person strong-arming him was holding something or someone over his head. They wanted to exchange the amulet for it. I don't know what it was, but I know he wouldn't have given up his chance at the Water Amulet."

"Do you love him?" Dromie asked quietly, looking over her shoulder to see if anyone was listening to their conversation.

Thess hesitated before answering, taking a moment to listen to her heart. She felt the unsteady beat throbbing in her chest. The pain made her ribs feel constricted. She did her breathing exercises to help calm herself. This was not the time to stress.

"I think I do. I've never felt this way before. I can't get him out of my thoughts. Being with him just felt... right. I think I even knew it when I saw him at the club the first time. Thinking of a future without him feels like torture," she sighed deeply, biting her bottom lip. "I can still feel him, even though I know he is not here. I miss his scent, his taste. Damn, I think I'm going crazy."

"Do you think you could be life mates?" Dromie asked curiously.

"Yes. Maybe. I don't know. I've never known a siren to take a life mate ever, but I can't imagine living the rest of my life without him," Thess replied, sighing. Her eyes turned to the ceiling as if the answers were written there. "I just wish I knew if he was okay."

"I think I may know a way to find out what's going on," Dromie said, glancing at her friend's bandaged up shoulder. A secretive smile flashed across her face as she rubbed another tear off Thess's cheek. "Stay strong, please. I got this. You just focus on the tourney."

Dromie ran out of the alcove and then went outside, transformed into her true waterbird form, and took off towards the skies.

Dromie ran into the club breathless while searching the room. There that bastard was. She stormed over to where Grif was leaning over a table sweet talking two wood nymphs. She glared at the nymphs causing the girls to scatter in the opposite directions before she grabbed his shoulder and forced him to look at her.

"Oh, hey, honey baby, how's it going?" His eyes briefly widened in shock before his face settled into a sultry smile, his eyes drifting down to the top of her breasts as her heavy breathing caused them to rise and fall.

"Don't you dare honey baby me you ass. Where. Is. Kage?" She emphasized each word by poking him in the chest.

"Kage? Why would I know? Do I look like his keeper?" He said as he shrugged, reaching over to grab his drink off the table.

She slapped the drink out of his hand. It bounced and spilled over his shoes. The glass shattered across the floor.

Grif looked down at his boots, frowning at the whiskey spilled on them. He was about to protest when she stood up on his toes and grabbed the front of his shirt.

"If you don't tell me where Kage is, or take me to him, you will regret ever taking a step in my uncle's club, and you will be banned from setting foot in here again. Do you understand me? I know everything. Including your part in it." She released him and pointed to the door. "We will talk on the way. Go."

"He.. he.. he's probably at his cabin or at the estate or something," Grif stammered as he followed her out the doors. The bouncers watched their every move, stepping closer to them.

He looked at her for a moment and blurted out, "I haven't seen him since last week, your guess is as good as mine. I have no clue what is going on or where he is at."

He turned his head down, then glanced up at her with his most sultry look, his amber eyes sparkling in the dim lights.

"Well, you're going to bring me to his cabin," Dromie stormed, more upset that he was trying to play her when she wanted to do what was best for Thess. "And if he's not there, you're going to drag your sorry ass with me to the estate or anywhere else he might be lurking until we find him. Thessie was injured yesterday in the tournament and the only thing she's asking for is him. She's not allowed to be seen by a healer until the trials are over, lest she forfeit winning, but she is allowed visitors. I'll be damned if I let him hurt her anymore than he already has by not bringing him to see her."

Grif sighed and Dromie stomped out the doors with Grif following hesitantly. She turned into her water bird form before grabbing Grif.

Kage was bent over on the patio, sweat dripping down his bare chest while he worked repairing the flooring. He glanced up when he heard a bird's cry followed by panicked yelling. He wiped the sweat from his brow and pushed his hair out of his eyes scanning the sky.

Kage watched as a halcyon raced towards the house clutching a large flailing object. As it got closer, he realized it carried Grif in its talons. The massive water bird dropped his friend on the ground causing him to land on his ass with a grunt while the halcoyn landed gracefully and transformed into Dromie. He stared at them in confusion.

Why would Grif have Dromie bring him here? He wondered.

If he had been in a better mood, he would have laughed at his friend being dropped on his ass. Instead, he was wondering what in the hell the two of them were doing at his house. He stalked down to the edge of the porch stairs.

"Sorry," Griff said with a sheepish grin as he dusted himself off and headed towards the porch.

"I don't care what you have to say," Dromie said as she marched up to the porch stairs, shoving Grif out of her way. "I don't care about your sorry excuses or explanations. Thess needs you and you need to come now. She was injured in the fight and she's not allowed to be healed until she either wins or forfeits. She wants you to be there for some ungodly reason." Grif grumbling, glaring at Dromie and rubbing his sore ass.. He stood there like he desperately wanted to be somewhere else and Kage didn't blame him.

"You better have a good explanation to why you just ditched her without a word by the time we get there," Dromie continued. "For that matter, why did you kidnap her to begin with? Forget that, you can explain that part later. For now, we need to get to the tourney," she said, poking him in the chest with her finger.

Kage stood there, immovable. His face showed no emotion. Then, a grin spread across his face and his eyes lit up. He watched as Dromie's eyes traveled up and down his body, he felt self conscious at how dirty he was with his sagging jeans and bare chest.

"As much as Thess might appreciate you being shirtless, if I have to present your ass to her entire clan of sirens, you better look semi-presentable. Now," she stomped her foot and pointed to a shirt tossed onto the railing of the porch before transforming back into her beast form.

"Wait, are you just going to leave me here?" Grif whined looking from his friend to the water bird, a look of astonishment on his face.

Kage smiled at his friend with a feral grin and shoved the hammer he was holding into Grif's chest.

"Why don't you make yourself useful for once." Kage arched an eyebrow then gestured at the porch before pulling his shirt over his head.

Dromie flapped her wings, taking flight from the ground before grabbing him around his biceps and lifting off towards the sky.

They landed outside the gates. Kage stared at the arena in awe for a moment. The white coliseum glistened in the moonlight. Dromie did not give him much time to look around. She transformed and ran in, heading toward the Thalassic clan gates. She motioned for Kage to follow behind her. As they approached the archway, the horn blared announcing the beginning of the final tournament.

"Hurry! She's already on the arena floor! The fight has already begun!" Dromie yelled behind her as she dashed down the long hall with Kage following on her heels.

174

When they entered the siren's alcove panting from their run, silence fell as all the sirens present turned to face the commotion they had made.

Talora glared towards the pair.

"Dromie, what the hell is this? And who is that?" She said pointing a finger.

"I don't have time to explain, but Thess had asked for him to be here. How is she doing?" She panted trying to catch her breath and push up to an open section facing the arena.

Dromie glanced at Talora. She knew that she could not harm him on the island. There were strict rules in place. Only combatants during the tourney could wage in battle.

They all turned their focus down to the floor as a clash of steel sounded throughout the area.

Kage stood in the middle of the siren's den, fearing this would be how it ended for him. Death by an entire clan of sirens singing. All the sirens took turns glaring at him. Thess's mother looked like she wanted to rip his heart out with her bare hands. He felt the animosity radiating from everyone in the alcove. His instincts kicked into high alert, warring between fleeing for his life or standing his ground and fighting for the bond he felt for Thess.

All thoughts of the sirens in the room vanished when he saw her. She stood in the arena, head held high, protecting her injured left arm. The bandage was soaked in fresh blood.

His heart ached as he realized how much he truly

missed her. His eyes surveyed every inch of her. Then the worry set in as he saw the other siren.

Chapter Twenty-Two

The final battle

Thess lifted her head high as she felt the throbbing in her left arm. It was a distraction she could not afford to have. Many sirens had lost their lives in this arena. She did not want to be one.

She curled her toes in the sand to find the rhythm of the water. The song was different from yesterday. More fast paced. The crowd must have worked the energy up.

She closed her eyes for a moment to grab focus.

Leucosia stood across from her. Her blue eyes spoke volumes. She could read the hatred for her there. She knew her mother had been right. Leucosia would not stop until she was dead.

Leucosia had changed weapons. In her arms today was a silver falcata sword. The sword was curved, single-edged, hook shaped and extremely deadly. She held the hilt of carved wood shaped into a seahorse. The curved

177

fish hook shaped blade looked deadly.

She steeled herself; it was time. The horn blew.

She waited to see if Leucosia would go on the defense or offense..Her cyclone spun towards her. Offense it was. She grabbed her sword and chanted her spell. The sword sliced it in half, pushing her back several feet.

Thess cast her song, steady and strong. A wave formed in front of her, crashing into Leucosia and knocking her down to her knees.

Thess felt a moment of satisfaction. She knew she had to stay away from Leucosia; she wasn't sure how well she would be in close combat fighting with her arm as it was.

She sent another wave crashing at Leucosia before she could gain her feet. Leucosia rolled to the side, the brunt of the wave barely catching her calves.

Leucosia cast a whirlpool spell and Thess felt the pull of the undercurrent dragging her feet towards it. She shoved further back, planting her feet in the sandbank.

Feeling the song start in her core and spread, she sang the spell, collecting all the water she could grasp. The arena grew colder and colder as the clouds above Leucosia swelled. Sheets of the ice storm crashed into her and around her, causing Leucosia to stop singing. The rising whirlpool came to a crash, sending small waves ebbing to all corners of the arena.

Thess took a deep breath, planning her next song. She knew there was no time for rest. Raising her arms above her head, she gathered her strength, grimacing against the pain in her left arm. She called her hurricane forth. The eyewall danced around her; she marveled before sending it crashing into Leucosia.

Leucosia blocked the brunt of the impact with a

water shield spell. She read the determination and hatred in Leucosia's eyes.

She didn't see the spell cast even as the wall of water knocked her down. She floated under water for a moment before hitting the ground. A cloud of sand billowed around her, blocking her vision. The wound on her left arm had come open as the surrounding water turned a murky pink, dyed with her blood. Her vision blurred, black spots dancing around the edge as she almost passed out from the pain.

Around her, she heard the echoing of a song. She glanced up and could see the amulet was glowing. She knew the song had come from it. Rolling over, she got to her feet. She cast a spell to create an ice wall before the next tidal wave hit her.

The spray of the water crashing into the ice wall and spraying her felt so cold. The pain in her arm distracted her from the battle. She took a deep breath, filling her lungs. Her blood dripped slowly into the water below her.

Thess tried to cast her next spell when Leucosia dove for her. She jumped to the side, barely missing the blade. She drew her sword, trying to figure out a plan to get away from the sparring. She blocked the blows coming at her. She felt her strength slowly slipping away from her every time her arm was jarred from a blow.

The blood was pooling in her left hand from her wound. She grabbed it, saying a quick spell to bind it with the surrounding water, and created a spear. She drove the spear at Leucosia with as much strength her left arm had.

Leucosia grabbed her face in shock and stumbled back as the spear grazed her cheek. Blood dripped from the wound on her face.

Thess saw the sword swinging towards her and

blocked it at the last moment. She fell back, almost tripping, but regained her balance and dove for Leucosia, bringing the sword down. Leucosia raised her falcata up, deflecting the hit but she fell from the force.

Thess kept driving, knowing if she stopped she could not start again. She would bring the sword down, then the spear. One after the other. The spear sliced Leucosia's chest; she yelled in agony.

Thess called forth for the water in Leucosia's veins. Just enough to weaken her. She would control it this time now that she knew more about what she was doing. The wound in her chest made it easier for the water to escape.

Thess met Leucosia's eyes and placed her blade on her throat.

"Do you concede?" she said.

"I will never concede," Leucosia growled as she kicked Thess in the groin.

Thess stumbled back in shock. Leucosia jumped and dove at Thess with renewed energy. It was Thess's turn to block. Her arm was aching. She could not even catch a breath to cast a spell. The spell holding her spear fell.

Thess dove out of the way of Leucosia's thrusting falcata. Rolling to the right, she gained space for a moment.

Thess heard the song in her head calling forth her hurricane. She sat in the eyewall trying to catch her breath for a moment, but she heard Leucosia trying to beat at the walls.

Changing the song, she added the ice crystal spell and the hurricane slowly turned into ice shards. Leucosia kept smashing her falcata at it but was doing no damage. Her strength was not enough to break through the wall of water and ice.

Thess grabbed the last of her power, grabbed

every droplet of water the hurricane had, every ice shard, and sent it crashing against Leucosia. She slammed into the arena wall, dizzy and confused after her head smashed into the stone.

Thess had never felt such power before. Walking up to Leucosia's sprawled body leaning on the stone wall, she rested her sword blade under her chin. Using the tip of the blade to lift her head, she met her cold and dazed eyes.

"You will concede this time." Her voice rang steady. Steadier then she felt.

"Finish me off," Leucosia said defiantly. "I have shamed my clan for the last time."

Thess watched as tears of rage filled Leucosia's eyes.

"Concede," Thess repeated flatly, ready to be done.

"Never." She spat in Thess's face, grimacing in pain, and placed a hand over the wound on her chest.

"Only cowards would choose a simple death over regaining their strength and trying again," Thess said quietly.

Leucosia stared at her. Thess watched as the fight slowly drained from her eyes. They were both weary from the years of training and the days of fighting. Leucosia sighed and raised her hand in concession. Thess looked in her eyes knowing the battle with her was over but the war was far from done. The crowd went wild. Thess stepped back, gladly hearing the horn announce the end of the tourney.

She made her way to the center of the arena, where the troll stood waiting. Her whole body ached and her temples throbbed. She had trouble focusing on her surroundings with the pain crashing in waves throughout her entire body.

"The winner of the tourney is Thessalia Potamides of

the Thalassic clan," the troll stated. "Please raise a cheer in honor of the new guardian of the Cyrene islands and the Amulet of Water."

A cheer rang through the crowd. Thess tried to enjoy the moment of victory, but pain was racing through her whole body. The troll raised up her good arm while the crowd bellowed their excitement. After some of the commotion died, he gently set it down, realizing her agony.

The three priestesses came to the arena floor, gliding on top of the water. Their dresses floated with them as they walked towards her. She looked at their beautiful faces in awe, noticing how the dresses never seemed to get wet, even as they stood on the water.

Thess felt the amulet before she even saw it. The song sang to her, calling her, reassuring her. A bit of peace washed over her as she knelt down. She noticed the center priestess was holding the amulet in her hands. It seemed to glow even brighter today.

The priestesses stopped in front of her. One touched the middle of her forehead and the other two touched her cheeks as they spoke the victory speech. Their hands felt warm and tender.

"Thessalia Potamides of the Thalassic clan," they said in unison. "You fought bravely and courageously in this battle to determine who should hold the guardian domain. Your spells were strong and true. Your clan shall continue to hold guardianship as it passes from Talora Potamides to you, Thessalia Potamides."

The two priestesses on the outside dropped their hands but the center one kept hers there.

"Your clan," the center priestess started, "should be proud of their champion. You are truly a brave and compassionate siren."

The last priestess dropped her hand, then she held the amulet up for all to see. "I present the amulet of water to our champion. May the blessings of Amphitrite be upon you, Thessalia, and your clan, as may these blessings be upon us all."

The crowd cheered as she held it aloft. She stood there a moment before bringing it down and gently placing it around Thess's neck.

Thess felt the warmth as the chain slid down the sides of her face. She looked down as the amulet rested on her chest. A strange feeling settled over her. A warmth spread throughout her body. The pain was gone, the tiredness was gone, and the warmth was all she felt.

She looked up as she started to rise and the crowd gasped.

Kage stood in the alcove, all awareness of the other sirens gone as he watched Thess. His heart stopped every time she took a hit. He could tell she was weary and in pain.

The fight was finally over; he sighed. Relief washed over him as he watched. She had won; she was still alive, but badly wounded. He wished they had let a healer attend to her before this ceremony.

He shifted anxiously to watch her as the priestess laid the amulet on her chest. The amulet shone bright, its blue diamond emitting a soft, bright light.

The priestesses stepped back in shock.

The light grew brighter and brighter. It shone throughout the stadium. Then, she lifted her eyes.

Thess's eyes glowed, along with the amulet. Her feet

started to rise from the sand bed to just above the water. Her toes scraping the surface. She looked like a goddess, floating above the pool. His heart stopped and his breath caught as he watched her.

The crowd was quiet, like no one had ever seen such an omen. Such a blessing. Kage was unsure of the meaning. Was it a sign of peace or a sign of war?

Thess heard the song in her head, her toes skimming the surface of the water before she was set back down and then it was gone.

The pain came rolling back all at once. She gasped from it, bile rising up in her throat. She set her eyes towards her alcove. Her mother stood there, blocking Dromie from entering the arena. Her eyes shone with pride. She took a deep breath, focusing on keeping her balance as darkness danced along the edge of her vision. It was all she could do to make the trek back on her own feet.

Thess walked the path back to them but stopped when her eyes met his. Kage was here. She felt her chest tighten and her breath hitch. Warmth flooded from her core to her cheeks as her eyes took him in. She stood transfixed for a second before the pain hit in another wave causing her to grimace. She forced her feet to continue walking, not taking her eyes off of him. He was there. All the questions came flooding back. There was so much she wanted to ask.

Dromie pushed past Talora as she spotted Thess making her way those last couple feet. She supported her as she walked back to the alcove.

"You did good," Talora stated. "But you let the battle rage on too long. Next time, be faster."

Thess stared at her mother a moment. Even in pain after winning the battle, she still found something to criticize.

Thess glanced to the side as Kage stood behind everyone, quietly waiting. Their eyes locked. Ehe tried to read the emotion in them but it was hard to focus. She knew Dromie dragged him here. A million thoughts ran through her head of everything she wanted to ask and say to him.

She felt the world start to spin out of control as she leaned further into Dromie's arms. The blackness blurred her vision until it was all that there was. She managed to whisper out one word before the darkness consumed her.

"Kage."

Chapter Twenty-Three

As Thess started falling, Kage scooped her up before she could hit the ground. Cradling her in his arms gently, he carried her through the halls to the clan's antechambers.

Dromie was fretting close behind them, with Nem following on her heels. Thess felt herself fade in and out of consciousness, catching glimpses of the hallways and her friends. She was hearing the voices surrounding her, but not understanding the words of their conversation.

Kage set her down in a chair. Dromie started picking at Thess's bandages, worrying like a mother hen. Nem was pacing back and forth, unshed tears shining in her muddy brown eyes.

Thess sucked in a deep breath as the fabric pulled at the clotted blood and open wound, her vision temporarily blurred again. The pain woke her momentarily from the darkness that surrounded her.

Her eyes locked with Kage's. She tried to stay calm. The pain felt so intense. Every nerve in her body sang with the pain coursing through her. She wanted to ask him questions, but could not catch even one thought that ran through her mind.

"Keep on breathing, Thess. Just making sure this is completely clean before I can heal you. Nem, don't just stand there like a gaping idiot. Hand me that jug of water from that table and the cloth napkins," Dromie directed, pointing down at the table.

Nem rushed to comply, setting the supplies on the table next to Dromie. Nem stepped back, trying to stay out of the way and twisting her hands together nervously.

Kage got down on his knees before Thess, taking her good hand in between his. He looked into her eyes, willing to distract her and wishing he could take away the pain as Dromie worked.

Nem paced behind them, trying to stay out of the way. Quietly, her eyes shifted from Kage to Dromie to Thess.

"Are you hungry?" Kage joked. "I can make you a peanut butter and jelly sandwich."

"You ass," Thess hissed through her teeth.

Dromie tugged on a bandage that had dried on her skin. Ripples of pain went through Thess. She squeezed Kage's hand tighter as a wave of nausea hit her. She closed her eyes, trying to take deep breaths until the pain subsided a bit.

"Do you have to be so rough, Drom?" Thess ground out between gritted teeth, trying not to flinch. She turned her eyes back to the male in front of her. Curiosity hit her, but the pain made it hard to focus.

"If you want to keep your arm, I'll do what I must," Dromie retorted, sponging out flecks of sand and debris from the wound bed. When she was satisfied that it was sufficiently clean, she glanced around before taking a few steps back.

Her body once again transformed, graceful wings of water forming behind her. She trembled, her body strained from using her magic to change forms so many times in such a short period of time. Barely managing to change into her shifter form, she raised herself onto the table next to her friend. She leaned her great head forward, her beck resting against the top of the wound as shimmering tears formed and rolled down into the wound bed. She held still, letting the tears fall as the skin knit itself back together slowly until all that was left was a faint silver scar that ran from shoulder to shortly past the elbow.

Dromie hopped off the table with a fluid grace, transforming back into her human form. She stumbled on her feet and stepped back, her head spinning from the effort of healing and transforming back and forth so many times. She took a couple deep breaths to calm the dizziness as she grasped the edge of the table.

"Dromie, are you okay?" Thess asked, whipping her head up to look at her friend. She marveled at the fact that her arm no longer ached.

"Yeah, I've just had a busy day and might have pushed myself a little too far," she said, laughing and holding her head while leaning on the table.

Nem reached out a hand to help steady Dromie. "Are you sure?" She said shyly.

Dromie nodded again, smiling at Nem.

"You were wonderful today, Thess," Nem said.

Thess smiled at her. "Thank you."

"We are all proud of you," Nem said, her eyes shifting nervously to Kage then back to Thess. "Are you feeling better now?"

"Yes," Thess said. She could see her mother waiting behind Nem. Anger radiated from every pore of her body. As she stood, her arms folded across her chest, her eyes cold and distant.

Talora took that opportunity to speak up, looking at the four of them gathered there, her daughter's hands between Kage's.

"I think we need to talk," she said harshly, her tone cold.

"Can we please have a moment to eat and rest before we get into this, Mom?" Thess retorted. She pushed herself up from her chair, looking down at her mother and putting Kage, Dromie, and Nem behind her.

Talora nodded with pursed lips. The sneer on her face showed the disgust she was feeling.

"Very well, but we will not put this off for long," she replied. She turned on her heel and walked away to stand with Asiris.

Thess stood up, marveling at the fact that she no longer felt faint. She flexed her left hand a couple of times, testing it out. The arm felt a little stiff, but otherwise it was like nothing had happened.

"Can I speak to Kage alone for a moment?" Thess asked Dromie and Nem.

"Sure," Nem said, reaching up to hug Thess. She glanced at Kage again, nervously, before walking over to sit by her mother.

"If you do one thing that upsets her…" Dromie said, stabbing a finger into Kage's chest.

Kage stared at her finger in his chest then looked back up at Dromie. "Got it."

Thess walked over to the food tables, piling food onto a plate as Kage stood behind her. He quietly followed her as she walked back down the hall to the arena alcove.

She sat down on the bench, then looked over at him.

"What happened?" She whispered. She tried to control the trembling in her voice.

"I took care of everything," he said, running a finger across her jaw.

"You still can't tell me anything?" She turned away, tears burning in her eyes.

"I…" he started, shaking his head. Jumping up, he paced the alcove anxiously, making the alcove feel so much smaller than it was. His stride was eating the ground up as he walked back and forth.

He stopped and looked down at her. She felt her heart jump to her throat as she stared into his eyes, losing herself in the dark pools.

She turned away in frustration, not understanding why he wouldn't tell her what was going on.

"I want to tell you everything," he started, his voice sounding husky. "I know if I say too much, it puts you in danger. I would never want to do that. Please, just be patient, at least for a while longer."

She glanced back up at him. Debating if she wanted the truth more right now or just to be with him. She sighed, turning her head away. Feeling so tired, plus, she knew a fight with her mother was brewing.

"I am tired," she said gravely. "For now, I will accept that, but soon I will want the truth. The entire truth. Do you understand?"

He nodded and then crouched down, bringing his face level with hers. Their eyes engaged as they stared deep into each other's soul.

"I missed you, my little siren," he rasped, before gently brushing his lips across hers.

She felt herself drift further into his spell. He nibbled her bottom lip. Sighing, she reached up to cup his face.

"I missed you too," she said before setting the plate of food aside. Reaching her other hand up, she cupped the back of his neck and then slid her hands up to run her fingers through his hair.

She felt herself dive further into the kiss as his mouth explored hers deeper. She had missed the taste of him. Missed the feel of his calloused hands as they gently ran along her skin. Missed the scent of cyprus that lingered on his skin.

He pulled back, kissing her on the tip of her nose.

"Eat up, little siren." He smiled as he handed the plate back to her. "You will need the energy later."

She laughed at him, shaking her head.

Nem and Dromie sat in the antechambers, quietly observing. Nem watched as Talora paced back and forth. She could hear her mother and Talora talking about Thess.

This was not good. After Thess won the tourney, they should have been happy. Everyone should have been celebrating her victory, but that obviously was not happening anytime soon.

Dromie had brought a male here and Thess was the one who had asked for him. The sirens were not authorized to talk to males, except when calling them forth for the goddess. They had drilled the lesson into them their whole life. When the time was right, a siren would choose a man to use, then get rid of him. They were never to be kept around, ever.

The few times they took Nem into town, she never talked to anyone if she could avoid it, except Thess and Dromie. She saw Thess talking to males from time to time, but that always seemed to be in passing.

Standing by him made her feel nervous and scared. She had never been around any males before. Other than when they occasionally took her into town for a meal or shopping. She had not even sung a siren call to someone yet. Her mom, Asiris, told her she was not ready.

She looked at Dromie wanting to ask questions about the male, but not wanting to take a chance that her mom would hear them talk.

"Thess is completely out of line," Asiris said angrily. "You need to get her under control. It is ridiculous that she thinks it is alright to keep a pet around."

"I know," Talora growled. "I will set her straight. She will do her duties for the clan and get rid of the male."

"She better. The clan will not stand for her parading this male through the village," Asiris grumbled, walking away from Talora.

Turning around one last time, Asiris said, "She has always been headstrong. I told you long ago to nip her behavior in the bud. You never did, and now we all pay for this."

Nem shivered. She hated dealing with her mother's anger. Most of the time she was so calm and serene, but when she snapped...

"I said I would handle this," Talora said, an icy rage simmering in her voice as she narrowed her eyes.

Asiris and Talora stared at each other angrily for a moment before Asiris walked off. Talora soon followed.

Now that her mother and Talora had left, she turned to Dromie.

"What's…" she started, then stopped. She wasn't sure how to ask. She didn't even know what she wanted to ask for sure. So many questions flooded her mind.

"What are males like?" Nem said, words tripping out of her. "Why would she want him around? Are they all as scary as he is? Why did you bring him here? How will he get home? What were you thinking?"

Dromie laughed, cutting off Nem's questions.

"No," Dromie said, giggling. "Not all males are scary. Just as each of us are different from each other, so are they. You don't need to be terrified of them. They should be more scared of us."

Dromie winked at Nem dramatically and paused thoughtfully before continuing. "Even standing up to the queen siren herself shows how brave Thess is. Bringing him here was the right thing because Thess wanted… no, needed him here. I think she wants him around. She might just be in love with him, even if she has not admitted it to herself. I think he might be her life mate. When you find your life mate, you'll do anything to be with them."

Nem opened and closed her mouth, no words coming through the shock. Thess was in love? She would never have thought it possible. Sirens don't fall in love, they don't talk about love. Love causes them to be weak. Sirens cannot be weak or they will not survive.

"Are you sure?" Nem stammered. Biting her lip nervously.

Dromie nodded.

Nem stared down at the floor, processing what she had seen and heard today. The truth she had grown up knowing versus the changes going on around her.

Chapter Twenty-Four

Thess, Kage, and Dromie made their way to the ship to head back to their cove. Talora stood at the top of the gangplank, arms akimbo as she waited for the trio to make their way on the ship. The rest of the clan, including Nem, was already on board and waiting for them to cast off.

As soon as they had boarded the ship, Thess knew Talora would not wait for any more explanation. She wished this didn't have to happen in front of everyone. She looked around, trying to find a suitable spot for the argument.

"Well?" Talora said, waiting for an explanation.

Thess took a deep breath, steadying her nerves before answering her mother.

"Mom, can we go somewhere that we can have some bit of privacy?" Thess gestured to the front of the ship.

They quietly made their way to the front, moving as far as they could get from the others.

"Mom, this is my… um… friend, Kage." She said, gesturing to him as they made their way further down the ship.

"Sirens do not keep male pets, let alone as friends," Talora replied, her eyes sweeping over Kage with disgust. "Especially not low life shifters. Don't think I didn't know what he was the moment he stepped into the room. The stench of the dirty swamp water permeates off his hide."

Kage stepped forward angrily, opening his mouth to reply, but was stopped when Thess reached out a hand to rest on his chest.

"You do not know him like I do," she replied to her mom. Glancing up at Kage, she hoped he would let her deal with her mom, no matter what insults she threw his way.

"As future leader of this clan, you need to uphold siren traditions. Even mingling with him is against our ways. You should know better," Talora scoffed. "Men are good for only one thing, then you dispose of them. So I can tell by your face it's time for him to go."

Thess took a moment to answer.

"I'm sorry, mom, I'm not like you." She reached out and grabbed Kage's and Dromie's hands, turning to head to the other end of the ship.

"Do not turn your back on me. I am not finished talking with you," Talora yelled against the wind. "I have let you push the boundaries of our laws, but this is going too far."

"This is my choice. I have fought for my clan and proven my worth. I love him," Thess declared, after turning to face her mother again. She paused for a moment as what she said sunk in. She could not look at him, fearing his reaction. "You just don't understand.

You have never understood me."

"You are more like me than you will ever know," Talora sighed as she closed her eyes. She rubbed the bridge of her nose in frustration.

"Before you were born, I met someone and thought I fell in love at first sight. I had done my duty as a siren for over 200 years and never felt the way he made me feel. We were banned from taking on relationships or bringing males to the village, just as we are are today. But I couldn't bear the thought of killing him, so I hid him in a cove miles from the village." Talora took another breath before meeting her daughter's eyes.

"Then, I found out I was pregnant with you. My mother had already made me give up one child, as they forbid us to keep male offspring. I started spending more and more time with him as you grew inside me. It overjoyed me not only to have conceived, but with the man I loved. Your grandmother was still the leader of the clan. She began questioning why I had been spending so much time at sea, neglecting my lessons and sneaking off just as you did. One day, she followed me to the cove where your father and I had started to build a home for ourselves. She went to do what I couldn't bring myself to and ended his life, our dreams."

Talora turned and stared out at the sea and the islands slowly being concealed by the mists as their ship sailed further away towards the mainland. Her eyes had a faraway look of deep sadness in them.

"It was an awful bloody battle," Talora said, her eyes gazing off distantly. "I tried to stop them, but your grandmother trapped me behind a wall of water that, despite my strength, I couldn't penetrate until it was too late. He had killed her. She was so busy focusing on separating us, she did not see the dagger he had in his hand. He had been so busy trying to save me. She delivered a crippling blow to him as she went down. By that time, others from our village had arrived and seen the horrors of this male killing their leader. I had no choice but to end his life or show weakness to the clan. There was no returning or convincing the others once they had seen the massacre. Now you must understand why we have the rules that we do. You cannot let your heart be governed by such a foolish emotion and jeopardize not only your own life but that of your family and clan. Males are good for one thing only, should the Goddess bless you with a child. Then, he is to be sacrificed in tribute to the goddess."

Thess stared at her mother in shock, processing the story. She wanted to know more about her father. He had not just been a stranger. All the times she had asked about him, Talora had known and chose not to answer. Plus, she had a brother. Where was he? Would Talora tell her more about him? She wanted to find him and bring him back.

Talora turned and walked a few steps away from the trio before saying over her shoulder, "He may accompany us as far as the shore, but he and Dromie must leave when we land, or you know what you need to do. They are never to set foot on our land ever again."

"Do you really mean it?" Kage whispered, his voice rough, as he turned to meet Thess's eyes. Gently reaching up, he cupped her cheek.

"Yes," she replied breathlessly. "I've known for some time, but I didn't want to admit it to myself or you. But, you came back for me…"

Kage held a finger to her lips before running it along her jawline and cupping her cheek.

Thess felt her whole body warm to his touch and his magic sang in her veins.

"Oh, my little siren. Only Cernunnos knows how much I have missed you. I felt empty without you these last days. Not a second goes by that I don't think of you. You belong to me, my little life mate." He wanted to kiss her right there, amongst other things. He stole a glance up to where her mother had just appeared at the other end of the ship and dropped his hand.

"I don't know what we are going to do. They'll kill you if you so much as step a foot near our village." Thess frowned and Kage could tell that she was contemplating her choices. She wanted to stay with her clan, but she wanted to be with him, too.

"You can leave and stay with me," he offered. His eyes locked with hers. He knew he did not have much to offer. Plus, with all he had done to her, she should refuse. He held his breath, waiting for her response, but Dromie chimed in.

"It's going to take a lot more than you just moving out, Thess. I wouldn't put it past your mother to hunt you both down and drag you back to the village kicking and screaming," Dromie said while frowning between the two of them.

Kage watched the emotions shifting in Thess's eyes as she contemplated what they talked about. Thess changed the subject, she turned back towards Kage.

"Kage, you said that you were being forced to steal the water amulet in exchange for the thing you most desire. Was that your family estate you were trying to get back? How did you get your homelands and estate back?

Dromie said that's where you were when she tracked you down," Thess said quietly as she peered up into his face. Dromie was standing beside her with a questioning look on her face.

Kage sighed, running a hand through his hair and closing his eyes for a brief moment before meeting hers again. He knew she would never let this rest.

"Before my mother died, she had secretly entrusted me with an amulet. She had said it had been in her family for generations and she begged me to keep it safe. It is just a family heirloom, a trinket, nothing more. I realized how I felt for you and when he threatened to send you to your mother in pieces as enticement for the water amulet, I knew I would give up anything to protect you. He didn't want my lands or house. He's been threatening to give them away for years, for fuck's sake. So I gave him the one thing I thought he would accept in exchange for the water amulet. Even if you would never speak to me again, I had to know I had helped protect you, even for a little while." He held his breath, waiting for her reaction.

"Oh, Kage, I don't know what to say." Her eyes glistened with unshed tears. Kage felt a tug at his heart looking into the glistening eyes.

Kage turned away from Thess glancing at Dromie. Dromie pursed her lips, glancing between the two of them.

"What did the amulet look like?" Thess whispered. Kage watched as they shared a terse look, the same feeling he had when he saw how excited Azazel had gotten.

"It's just an amber stone cradled in gold branches," Kage said, straightening his back. He remembered the look of excitement when Azazel saw the amulet. A feeling of apprehension clutched at his heart.

"That sounds like it might be the earth amulet," Dromie said, glancing at Thess.

"But Kage, don't you know the stories of the amulets?" Thess said, reaching out to run a finger across his cheek. "The amulets are more than just family jewelry. They held the essence of our tribes in them, the raw magic of our clans. It keeps our magic strong. But they also serve another purpose, which is why no clan has ever held onto more than one amulet."

Thess reached down, drawing the amulet on its long chain out from under her dress. The blue diamond pulsed with power in time with her heartbeat and had a faint glow emanating from it.

"There were seven amulets of power, each given to a clan or tribe to protect. When all seven amulets are brought together to the temple hidden in the waters of the Triangle of Bermuda, an ancient sea monster can be summoned to destroy the world."

"Who did you give it up to?" Dromie asked. All laughter left her eyes.

"A water demon named Azazel," he said, reluctantly. He looked down at his shoes. His mother had never explained it to him. Just insisted he keep it safe.

"I don't know what he is planning, but it can't be good if he's plotting to steal the amulets. We have to warn the other clans," Thess said as she clutched the amulet tighter in her fist.

"It seems we will need to find a way to rescue your amulet of earth too, Kage," Dromie said as she turned to him. "If you are the remaining heir of the Mistbright clan, it is your duty to lead the shifters and protect the amulet."

"Who's going to believe a siren, a water bird, and a crocodile shifter that a water demon is trying to steal the amulets of power and possibly use them to raise a mythical water beast?" Kage frowned, looking between the two girls. "Let alone trying to steal back the amulet from him would be suicide."

Chapter Twenty-Five

Watching as the shore came into view, Thess knew there was not much time left to decide. Did she stay with her mom or go with Kage? She twisted at the idea of having to choose between two people she loved. Tradition or love? She wondered.

Her eyes darted around the boat. She looked up at her mom, then at Kage.

She closed her eyes, trying to listen to her heart. What does my heart want? She asked herself.

When she opened her eyes, she met Kage's gaze. She felt herself drift away in the dark waters of his eyes. It was then that she realized there was never a choice. She would follow him to the ends of the earth.

She sighed. "Dromie, Kage, I want you both to head to your homes when we dock. Don't ask questions. Just go home, please. I will talk to you both soon."

Dromie opened her mouth to protest, but Thess shook her head.

Kage reached up, his hands sliding under her hair

202

to rub her neck.

"When will I hear from you?" He said softly, worry filling his eyes.

"Soon." She smiled, looking up at his face. She reached up and traced her finger along his scar. One day, she would have to learn the story of how he got that scar.

The trip felt like it took days, but was only an hour. Thess felt torn between being anxious to get off the boat and not wanting the trip to end. She looked out to sea, watching the sandy shores edge closer and closer.

She dreaded the moment her mom would find out what path she had chosen. Two weeks ago, she thought her mom would not care. Today she knew that wasn't true, but she needed to follow her heart. It said that traditions needed to change. She needed to change. Hopefully, one day, her mom would understand and forgive her.

The boat docked. Thess waited till everyone had left before unboarded with Dromie and Kage. She hugged Dromie goodbye.

She looked deep into Kage's eyes and traced his lips with her fingers. "Soon," she whispered.

He nodded, reaching up as he smoothed her hair down and then walked away to jump in the car with Dromie. He was so big in her tiny car. Thess laughed at them.

She went to the temple and placed the amulet back on the pedestal. She missed it already. Lovingly, she caressed the amulet as it sat on the altar. She knew she would miss it even more when she left. Her whole life she had heard that gentle lullaby and now she was not sure when or if she would hear it again. A tear rolled down her cheek. She knew her mother would never let her near it again once she knew the decision she had made. She wondered if Talora would even let her come back to the village.

Slowly, she strolled through the town, looking at all the homes. She wanted to remember it all, down to the last grain of sand. She looked at all the faces, memorizing her cousins and fellow sirens. It was so strange knowing she might never see any of them again.

She watched as Nem entered her house with Asiris. She hoped she would come to town to visit her.

She walked up the steps to the home she had shared with her mom her whole life. Sadness washed over her. She would miss this small home. She stared at the door, nerves making it hard to cross the threshold. Her hand reached out and twisted the knob tentatively. She saw her mother pacing the living room.

"I know that was hard," Talora started. "But it was the right thing to do. One day…"

Thess went to her room, shutting the door behind her. She did not have it in her to deal with her mother after the days events.

"Thess," Talora started from the other side of the door.

Thess turned the radio on and turned the volume up. She just didn't have it in her to listen to the speech. She had listened to her mom give enough speeches for a lifetime or two. Once she knew her mom was gone, she turned the radio off.

Tears streamed down her face. This was the last time she would be here. She would never have to sneak out. Laughing sadly to herself, she looked around her room. She would never again stare at the ceiling daydreaming about the world. She would be out there living her life and making her own choices. Shaking the thoughts off, she got to work.

She threw the things she wanted to keep on the bed. She had no luggage to pack her belongings in since she had never traveled far from home. They had never gone on a vacation and never left the village, so there had never been a need for suitcases. If she hadn't snuck out, she would not know of the outside world. The time with Kage was the longest she had ever been away.

When her mom finally went to her room, she grabbed her bags and started packing. Realizing just how little that she had, it didn't take long to gather all that she needed.

The sun was setting when she looked out her window. She glanced at the ocean, watching the orange, blues, and reds that splashed across the sky reflect on the surface of the water. Soon, the stars sparkled in the night sky.

Sighing, she threw her bags out the window. She climbed out, trying to be as quiet as she could. This was the last time she would sneak out of this window. The path to her car was dimly lit, so she walked it mostly by muscle memory.

Tossing her belongings into the trunk, she hopped in the car and drove off. She went to Dromie's little apartment first. It was a couple of blocks away from The Wave.

When Dromie opened the door, the floodgates opened. They sat there talking and crying for a while before Dromie gave her directions to Kage's home.

She drove up to the dilapidated house. She could see that it was being worked on, but it still had much to be done. Kage stood on the porch with his hands in the front pockets of his jeans. His jeans hung low and she admired his abs. The car headlights reflected off his bare chest and made his eyes shine red. A shy smile crossed his face as he boyishly watched her.

A feeling of peace settled in her soul as she jumped out of the car and ran into his waiting arms. He crushed her in his embrace. His lips crashed against hers. It felt like an eternity since she last felt him. It was as if she had been adrift at sea until she was with him again. She clung to him as the waves of desire hit her.

For a moment he pulled away. "It's not much right now, but I will get it fixed up for you."

Looking up at him, her heart melted. "I know we will."

He scooped her up and carried her into the living room. A mattress was laid on the floor with some blankets and a small fire flickered in the fireplace.

It feels cozy; she thought.

He laid her down gently on the bed before laying next to her. His finger traced her jaw slowly, sliding down her neck, along her collarbone. Then he slid his hand around her neck, bringing her face to his. His lips followed her jawline, nibbling gently.

"I love you," he whispered, before devouring her mouth.

She sighed. "I love you, too."

Kage pulled back, staring deeply into her eyes. Thess knew what he would see. Sadness. Tiredness. Love.

"Are you alright?" Kage gently brushed her hair out of her face.

She sighed, shook her head, then nodded.

He laughed softly. "I am here for you, no matter what."

A tear slid down her face. He pulled her close and held her until she slept.

Kage sat there, admiring her as she slept. The soft light of the morning sun rays coming in through a broken window made her skin glow. He watched as her chest rose and fell with each breath.

The fragility of her face was so deceiving. He thought back to how fiercely she had fought in the tourney. He kissed her forehead gently before climbing out of bed.

Kage headed up to the master bedroom, deciding it would be the first room he fixed up. Thess deserved a bedroom, he mused. He started cleaning up the broken furniture and debris off the floors.

"Need any help?" Thess said from the doorway.

Smiling up at her, he took her in, his eyes sliding from head to toe. She had his t-shirt on and nothing else. He could see the shadows of her areolas peeking out from under the white fabric.

"Yes," he said, walking over to her. His hand slid around her neck, pulling her mouth to his. After a moment, he gentled the kiss, slowing the rhythm. He nibbled at her lips, breathing her in.

He smelled the snakey bastard before he heard him. Grif. He pulled back from Thess with a sigh of disappointment.

"Hey," Grif said happily.

"Go away," Kage growled.

"Is that the way you talk to your most loyal friend, your brother, practically?" Grif laughed.

"Go away," Thess sighed, giving Grif the evil eye.

"As your future brother-in-law, I am offended." Grif winked at Thess. "I see you're fixing my bedroom up. So kind of you guys. I appreciate all your hard work."

"Get the fuck out!" Kage yelled half-heartedly. "No way in hell this is going to be your room."

Thess looked at Grif. "You're not man enough to take the room from me."

Grif laughed. Kage pushed Thess behind him, realizing once again how little she was wearing.

"Grif, go out front. Give us a few minutes," Kage said.

The snake shifter meandered down the stairs. Kage waited till he heard the front door shut.

"You might want to put some more clothes on." His eyes caressed her body lovingly.

She blushed and looked down and laughed. "Alright."

She went to her bag in the living room to dress while Kage went out front.

"What's going on?" Kage whispered as he approached Grif. He sensed by the way Grif paced and slithered around the driveway that something was wrong.

Grif was halfway down the driveway by the time Kage caught up to him. The laughter left Grif's face and he could see anger had replaced it.

"Talora came into town," Grif said quietly. "She is on a rampage looking for you guys. No one has told her anything, but it's just a matter of time. How are we going to handle this?"

"I'll talk with Thess," Kage said, sighing. "Maybe we should avoid town for a while. I'll send you a list of things to pick up for the house. I'll have it for you in a few minutes if you can wait around."

Grif moaned dramatically. "Do I look like your errand boy?"

"I'm pretty sure you've looked like my bitch our whole life," Kage laughed.

Grif punched him in the arm. "I am glad you're

happy. You deserve to be. I've always worried about the fact that you were such a loner."

Kage looked away, his eyes scanning the swamps. "No need to worry about me. I'll be fine. You, on the other hand..."

They were both laughing when Thess came out. She smiled at them.

"We need to make a list of things for Grif to get in town," Kage said.

"Alright, I have a few things I would like him to pick up," Thess said.

They sat there making a list for Grif before he drove off.

Kage waited till Grif's tail lights faded away. Looking down at her, he debated if he should tell her or not.

Sighing, he knew he could not keep more secrets from her. "Your mother was in town looking for us."

Thess sat there looking into the swamp quietly for a moment before glancing up at him.

"I will handle it," she said quietly.

Kage nodded. The pain in her eyes tore at his heart, tore at his soul, especially knowing he had a hand in causing it. Brushing a hand through her hair, he attempted to comfort her the best he could.

Thess sat looking out her car window, knowing she had to get out of the car and head into the village. Dread filled her at the idea of confronting her mother. Emotions were racing through her, anger, fear, and frustration. Taking a deep breath, she finally opened the car door.

Walking the familiar path, she felt a pang of nostalgia. She would miss seeing her sisters, cousins…

And even my mom every day. It was almost funny; she thought. It felt like a lifetime since I've been here, but it has only been a day.

Hearing the whispers, she knew they had noticed her. Talora ran up, a storm of anger brewing in her eyes.

"You've come home with your tail between your legs," Talora said, triumphantly. "I told you men weren't worth much."

"Stop searching for me," Thess said. She straightened up to her full height. She stared down at her mother, knowing she needed to stand her ground now or she would never be able to be herself.

Looking at Talora, she realized how much of herself she had hid. How she tried to be the dutiful daughter so much and only occasionally sneaking out to discover herself.

This was the first time she felt free. She would not spend her life living the way her mother had chosen for her. She was going to live on her own terms.

"You could treat me like an adult and not like a child you have to always control," Thess said calmly. She turned and walked back up the beach, her heart feeling a little lighter. She smiled to herself, amazed that she had stood up to her mom.

Chapter Twenty-Six

Thess flicked her tail into the air from the shallows of the swamp, splashing droplets of water towards Kage. He stood on the land; the moonlight glistened in his eyes as he laughed softly. He had his hands tucked into his pockets as he watched her with a predator's gaze, his eyes never leaving her. She moved her body forward to a kneeling position to pull herself closer to land.

"We could go for a swim instead of heading into town and mingling with everyone there," Thess said as she willed her magic, imagining her soft teal scales transforming into smooth pale legs. The pain of transformation flashed for a brief moment. Her wet skin prickled from a breeze that blew across her as she lifted herself from the ground. The moonlight and water were the only things touching her skin. The water drops sparkled like diamonds in the radiant light.

Kage let out a low growl, letting his eyes slowly trace from her head to her toes. The gaze left a smoldering warmth that spread out from her body. Every place his eyes touched, heat radiated from.

"I have to admit, you look good in legs." He smirked, the corners of his lips tugging up. Restlessly, he removed his hands from his pockets, brushing them through his hair, but it fell back haphazardly over his eyes, making him look more rakish.

Thess looked down at her naked body. Searching around, she picked up the dress they had thrown aside earlier. It had caught on a nearby branch. She slid into it, the backless white satin fabric clinging to her damp body.

"I think you forgot something," he said. His eyes met hers. A secret, seductive smile spread across his face. "Though I can stand here and look at you for all eternity."

He reached out a hand, gently sliding it across her lower back, leaving trails of heat where his calloused skin brushed hers. He leaned his head towards her ear, his warm breath caressing and tingling as he whispered. "If I had my way right now, you'd be forgetting more than just your shoes."

His left hand came up slowly, teasing the thin sleeves of her dress over her shoulder, baring it to the moonlight that showed off the top of the silver scar that ran to her wrist. He slowly kissed his way down her neck and shoulder, his hand dropping lower to caress her breast through the fabric, his fingers toying with her nipple. She arched into his touch, warmth spreading from her core outwards, her mind dizzy at the sensation coursing through her.

Kage took in a deep breath, smelling her arousal mingling with the lingering scents of the swamp. He met her gaze as he slowly let go of her, a mischievous twinkle in his eyes as he slid her sleeve back into place. He bent down and picked up her sandal.

"We wouldn't want to be late now, would we? Late

to your own celebration party. Andromeda would be disappointed," he said as he nipped at her earlobe before leading her back towards the road where her car was parked.

"Although, if you keep looking at me like that, I might just devour you here in the car and claim you, so no other male thinks twice about setting their eyes in your direction." His eyes met hers, heat simmering in the depths of their gaze.

He opened the passenger car door, turned, and picked her up by her waist, setting her in the seat facing him. His hands slowly drifted down her thighs to her knees. His fingers skimmed under the hem of her dress, making their way slowly back up her inner thighs while spreading her legs. He knelt down and chuckled as he dragged a tongue along her left thigh, his warm breath caressing her.

"It looks like you forgot something else, little siren."

Thess moaned, leaning back against the center console, her breath coming out in slow, ragged gasps as his tongue darted forward to the nub of her clit. His finger gently penetrated her, pushing into her wetness in a motion like the rocking of the boat out to sea. Her whole body felt the flames dancing inside her, building up to a crescendo as she rode his fingers and mouth. The silky fabric of her dress rubbing on her nipples made them harden. He paused, letting out a deep predatorial growl that sent gooseflesh across her skin.

"Please Kage, don't stop," she panted, her breasts heaving with every breath.

"Oh trust me, my little siren, I'm going to make you orgasm more times than there are stars in the sky." He slid a second finger inside her, gently feeling her softness squeezing in response. She whimpered his name and crested the wave of pleasure. His fingers slid out and he tasted her on his hand. Her scent filled the surrounding air. His eyes locked with hers, burning a dark, molten fire

"But first, I'm going to get you to your party before Andromeda skins me and displays my crocodile hide as her new clutch and boots," he chuckled.

Closing her legs, he pulled her soft, silky white dress back over them. He reached over, gently guided her body into the car. Then he buckled the seatbelt across her chest and waist before walking over to the driver's side and starting the motor.

By the time they pulled up to the club, her heart had stopped racing. She could see Dromie standing in front of the doors, bouncing up and down, waving madly as she saw them park. Before she had time to get out of the car, her best friend had bounded down towards them and pulled open the door, giving her an enormous bear hug.

"It's time to celebrate your victory. I knew you could do it! I never had any doubt you would hand those bitchy sirens their asses. Although you could have given me less heart attack watching you, but enough of that. You're practically glowing! We've mixed up a special cocktail just for you, The Sea Bitch! And there are presents, cake, food and more!" Dromie turned and gave a little wave to Kage before pointing to the front door. "Don't you try to sneak off! I know how much of a lone wolf you can be. You have every right to celebrate with us, too. I haven't seen my TT so happy until she met you."

Barring his sharp teeth, Kage growled at Dromie

jokingly. "I'm not a wolf, but I'll let the insult slide this once."

Thess felt the warmth creep up into her cheeks as Kage walked up beside her, sliding a warm palm across her bare back as they followed Dromie through the front doors of the club. There were balloons and streamers everywhere from the dance floor to the VIP lounge area. Every one of their friends seemed to be gathered for the celebration. Theo waved at them from the bar where he was leaning over, talking to the bartender as she lifted her hands, shaking a cocktail shaker vigorously before popping the lid off and pouring the shimmering turquoise liquid into the waiting coupe glasses without spilling a drop.

"Kage! Thess! Dromie!" Grif waved as he made his way over to the group with a big grin on his face. He walked up, grabbing Kage in a constrictive hug.

Dromie turned, storm clouds brewing in her eyes as she met Grif halfway across the floor and slapped him across the face, leaving four slight scratches where her nails had partially transformed into her talons.

"HOW DARE YOU, GRIF!" she screeched, standing on her tiptoes to look him in the eyes. She grabbed his shirt and pulled him close. Their noses touched as she clutched at him.

"I still have a bone to pick with you," she whispered heatedly. Tightening the grip on his shirt, she continued. "I still have not forgiven you for lying, manipulating me, and tricking me. How dare you trick me while you and Kage kidnap my best friend, then lie directly to my face when I ask for your help in finding her? Leading me in a fruitless search, feeding me false clues. You are lucky not a hair was hurt on her head and she found her life mate. If there was any other outcome to this story, the two of you would not be standing here alive today."

Her eyes turned molten blue as she smiled wickedly, her voice lowering.

"Luckily for you, I'm in an excellent mood, but if you so much as slither one foot out of line, you will find yourself a very sorry snake indeed." She emphasized the last sentence by raking her claws down his chest before giving him a shove and turning her back to him. "I could use a new snake skin bag."

Thess turned around and saw Nem. She ran up and hugged her. Surprised that Dromie was able to get her to come out. Nem never went to the club with them when they snuck out.

Thess turned around and saw Nem. She ran up and hugged her.

"I miss you so much!" Thess exclaimed.

"I miss you, too!" Nem said, squealed back. "It has been so lonely in the village without you. Everyone is so humdrum. They just train and are blah, so boring. Talora has been on a rampage, making sure we all train night and day. It's like she is preparing for a war. Miss Kaliegh is talking of retiring. She had gotten…"

Thess listened intently to Nem tell her all that was going on in the village. She knew there was nothing she could do to help her for the time being. She sighed and noticed Kage hiding at a corner table by himself.

She had hoped that more of her clan would sneak off and join the festivities. Become a part of the world instead of hiding in the village for all time. That was a far-fetched hope though, and at least Nem had shown up.

"Come over and actually meet Kage," Thess said, grabbing Nem's hand. She had decided that for tonight it was best to relax and worry about her clan tomorrow. "You did not get to be properly introduced to him before."

"Kage, this is my cousin Nementeia or Nem." Thess said.

All of a sudden, the crowd went silent. Thess looked at the door as Talora walked into the Wave. She stroud into the middle of the dance floor. Thess felt her nerves tighten, knowing her mom was here for a fight. She had hoped she would let things go, but should have known better.

She walked up to her mother. "What are you doing here?"

"You are standing here," Talora said, her gaze derisive, as her eyes traveled up and down Thess. "You are partying with strangers after you abandon your family, your clan. Is this the life you really chose?"

Talora's eyes shifted over to Nem. "You…" her eyes narrowed. She turned back to Thess, pointing in Nem's direction. "Not only do you demean yourself, but you drag your cousin into the swamps with you. You drink and party, act irresponsible. This is the life you want, a life of excess."

Talora's lips curled in disgust. Her gaze went back to Nem, staring at her niece with revulsion and disappointment.

Thess stood there, no words escaped her lips. She stared at her mom in disbelief.

"Talora," Dromie started. "We were just celebrating Thess's victory. A victory you and your clan shared. She had worked so hard and…"

Talora turned her rage at Dromie, cutting off her words. "You had your roll in all of this." Talora pointed a finger at her. "She would not have gotten into this mess without your influence. Since the day she met you, all you have done is teach her frivolities. You are a creature who lives a flippant life. I should have ended this…"

Thess moved between them, cutting off her mother's tirade. "I make my own decisions. We will discuss this tomorrow. Now leave."

Thess pointed to the door, stomping her foot in frustration. She stood staring down at her mom, using every inch of her height to intimidate her. She lowered her voice threateningly. "I said leave."

Anger flashed in Thess's eyes as she glared at her mother. She had hoped that her mother and her relationship had changed, but it obviously had not.

Talora looked like she wanted to say more, but she just stood there a moment glaring at her daughter before turning and storming off.

Chapter Twenty-Seven

The dawn sun creeped over the sands and ocean casting it in rich, warm colors. Thess and Kage cautiously approached the siren village. She had asked him to stay home, begged him to. He had refused to let her face her mother on her own. She looked up at her mate's face and watched the steely determination sharpen his features as he gently gave her hand a squeeze.

As they approached the village, she could see her mom standing in the middle of the buildings. A few other sirens were standing behind her. Talora stood there immobile as a statue, her head held high. Ready for battle, Thess thought.

The crown of their clan rested on Talora's head. Silver intertwined around five aquamarine jewels around its edge. The biggest jewel, a princess cut aquamarine, stood in the center surrounded by silver filigree shaped like ocean waves. The morning light shining through it made it come to life, looking like a star in the smooth velvet sky.

Talora was dressed in a regal purple toga which

accentuated her figure. Her hair was pulled back into a topknot. Every detail she had chosen, from the location to her outfit, was to make sure Thess knew who was in charge and what she had to face. Talora's brown eyes were staring daggers at Thess and Kage as they made their way through the sand towards the clan buildings.

Thess glanced down at her skirt and old ratty t-shirt, feeling underdressed for what she was about to face. She pushed the thoughts away, knowing that now was not the time to worry about such superficial details. Knowing Talora was battle ready, Thess hoped her mom would not attack Kage. She did not want to have to fight her mother, that day or any other, for that matter. She knew she would defend her mate if her mom came after him.

Thess paced her breathing while willing her nerves to steady. She took a deep breath in, held it, then slowly released it. She needed to stay calm if she was going to accomplish anything today.

Thess stared into her mother's eyes, the anger and frustration hitting her like a rock. She didn't wait for her mom to start scolding her, here in front of Kage and the sirens. She heard footsteps in the sand and felt the tension in the air like a storm about to break as more sirens made their way towards them. After last night, she knew she could not let her mother's ideas and opinions rule her life.

Deep down, she knew that her mom loved her, but she could not live the life Talora had chosen for her. After having spent so much of her life listening to this woman lecture her about every decision she made or did, it was time she chose her own way. This was her life to walk through, and she knew now where she was heading.

She released Kage's hand and pointed a finger towards Kage. Her body was ridged with anger and determination as she faced her mother. Taking a breath, she braced herself.

"I do not care about our people's history when it comes to this." Thess raised her voice. She sounded steadier than she felt. "He is my life mate. Whether you will accept that or not is no longer a consequence or concern to me."

Talora opened her mouth, looking like she wanted to speak, but Thess raised her hand, sweeping it towards the gathering sirens before she continued.

"Look at our clan!" Thess said. "Have a good look. We may be strong, but our numbers are dwindling. Not only are fewer sirens born every year, but many have left, never to be seen again. Don't you ever wonder why they leave and why they never come back? Look at the world surrounding us. Times are changing, people are evolving, and the tides are turning. If we don't change with it, we will just become another piece of fabled history. Just like the clan of Aerwyna."

Thess stopped, waiting for Talora to interrupt, but she did not. "For as long as I can remember, you have drilled into my head that one day I will lead our clan. One day, I will be the role model for future sirens to come. I am stepping into that role, yet you question every decision I make with your attempts to stick to traditions." She took a deep breath, gesturing to her friends, fellow sirens and then the temple that held the amulet.

"I have won my place in our clan, making our community stronger. You have sacrificed, others have sacrificed, but the time to stand together is now. We will be stronger people if we work together."

"There is a larger enemy we face now," Thess sighed and looked into Kage's face before continuing. "Azazel, a water demon, has at least one of the seven amulets of Calpa. He tried to take the amulet of water from us by trickery and deception. We cannot show weakness now. We must band together, not just our clan, but the other clans. Show a united front against an enemy coming for us all. We cannot do that if we are fighting over traditions."

"You may not understand my choice in male now, but I hope in time you will understand what I see in him." She stepped back towards Kage, gently locking her fingers with his again. "If you and the rest of the clan cannot accept these facts, then I don't know if I can stand being here another moment"

Her mother crossed her arms, her lips pursing in disapproval, but she looked around at the clan, half their eyes eager and interested, the others uncertain and wary. She stood at a crossroads, with two options in front of her.

"You, my daughter, are ever stubborn as the force gale wind. Do you think that tradition can be bucked because you want some male?" She gestured towards Kage.

Thess looked at her mom. "Kage is not some male. He is the one I am going to spend the rest of my life with. He is my life mate. You need to accept this, or I will leave to never return. That is a decision for you to make."

Talora stood staring at her daughter. She knew she had to choose between her daughter or tradition. She thought how her life would have been different if her mother had given in to her wanting of her mate.

Would she and Thess's father have been happy together? She mused.

She had been so miserable these last few weeks without her daughter. Did she choose tradition and lose the person she loved most in this world or accept this fate her daughter had chosen for herself? She sat there staring at the two, knowing her daughter would not back down. She could see herself in those eyes before she had lost hope.

Talora looked past the other sirens at the gentle rise and fall of the waves. Even the water's song changed over the years. Maybe it was time for her to change, for the clan to change. It wouldn't be easy, but it may be in the clan's best interest.

If they were going to war, she would prefer having her daughter by her side. Both fighting and to watch over her in battle. Looking back at Thess, she searched her face, looking for any sign that she would back down. The steeled determination that radiated from her daughter's face told her there was none.

"I do not like this at all. I'm not quite sure if I even like him." She put emphasis on the word him glaring icily at Kage. "However, you make a valid point. I will not stand in your way in the matter of your… mate. You have also rightfully won the respect of the clan and have earned your place as its leader. However, will you abandon our village or force him to leave his home? How will the others feel who have spent hundreds of years without a male in the village? Have you thought about how the others of our clan feel?"

Talora watched as Thess grabbed the male's hand. She wished she could change the path her daughter had chosen but knew she could not.

"I know change will not be easy. I plan to spend my time split between my duties here and with my mate in our new home. With the water's powers coursing through my veins, travel and communication between the two will never be an issue. Plus, you can always get a cell phone, Mom." Thess grinned at her. A gentle grin asking her to open her heart up.

Talora reached up and lovingly caressed the aquamarine studded crown on her head. She had held that crown longer than most. She had fought countless battles to defend it, both internally and externally. The path she had chosen had not been easy, just as the path Thess was choosing would not. She had always wanted her daughter to step up and rule. It seems Thess had done this, even though she disagreed with the decision and the way she planned to rule.

Maybe it was time that she pass it on and let the next generation rule. Bittersweet, she removed it. A glimmer of tears briefly shimmering in her eyes as she walked to her daughter, gently placing the crown upon her head, then kneeling down on one knee.

One by one, the rest of the clan followed suit, placing a glistening droplet of tears on her forehead. When the last siren had finished, Thess felt her forehead tingle with warmth.

Thess cleared her throat as she glanced around at her clan and her friends that had gathered. She smiled as she had their attention.

"I have a few suggestions I would like to initiate. First, while I would like to keep up the siren's traditions,

I propose that we discourage the drowning of sailors in our water, instead using our gifts to help our people prosper."

A few whispers started up, but as she looked across the gathered crowd, a hush descended.

"Secondly, I propose that should a siren child wish to attend school with the other magical creatures, they should be free to do so. It would give our clan a chance to expand our own knowledge. Plus, it would only strengthen our bonds with the other tribes if we were to mingle and create more friendships, like I have with Dromie and Kage." She smiled up at Kage. He and Dromie were her calm in this storm.

"And lastly," she said, taking the crown from her head. "I propose we start a council to govern the clan instead of one matriarch."

She laughed as she handed the crown to the priestess, Asiris, standing next to her mother. "Please, let us display this. It is one of our treasures. It belongs in the temple where the amulet is held."

"Those are some strong changes you wish to make, Thessalia," Talora replied while pursing her lips. "But if the others are in agreement, we can start first by creating a counsel. Then we can start putting your plans and others into motion. If I make a suggestion, however… You should bring in one member from the five families to be a voice on your new counsel."

"Perfect." Thess turned to the gathered sirens. "Speak to your mothers, daughters, and cousins. Decide which among your houses will represent on the counsel. We will meet one week from now. There has been enough excitement in the last few days that we all need rest. I shall return then. If you have a need before, then you can call me."

She turned back to Kage, linking her arms through her mates. They turned around and walked back through the sand to the parking lot where they had left his motorcycle.

"Well, what now do you suppose?" Thess asked as she pulled the helmet over her head.

"I would say you've stirred up enough trouble. You'll have those old sirens squabbling over it like hens," Kage said, helping her with the chin strap. He put his helmet on and jumped on the bike with her.

They drove off towards their home. Thess hugged Kage close on the windy roads.

Chapter Twenty-Eight

Looking up after taking an order, Cordie watched as Thess and Dromie made their way to their preferred table in the VIP section, one of the tables she was covering for tonight. Smiling to herself before nodding to the couple in front of her, asking if there was anything else they needed. Turning, she headed towards the bar to put in their order. Over the last weeks she had gotten to know Dromie, as she helped her find her friend. It would be nice to catch up and see how Thess was doing after everything that happened.

Making her way back towards her tables, she saw both the girls stand up and wave towards the crowd. Her eyes were drawn towards the figures approaching their table. She felt her heart speed up in her chest. Her cheeks burned as she spotted two males laughing and joking next to him. Theo, his blue eyes sparkling in the light as he ran a hand through his thick, blonde hair. She felt the tug in her heart when seeing him followed by the stab of pain.

She ducked behind the nearest pillar, taking deep

steadying breaths to calm her nerves. She hadn't spoken with him since that painful night when she was sixteen years old, and tonight she didn't feel like starting. He had been showing up at the club randomly for the last couple weeks. She managed to avoid him for years and now she could not escape him.

I will just have to meet up with Thess and Dromie another evening, she thought, sighing.

Spotting Saffron, the new girl, helping run the VIP section, she made her way quickly to her and pulled her aside.

"Is there any way that you can cover table two for me tonight? I'll take any table you want." Cordie tried to keep the pleading note out of her voice as Saffron looked over to the now gathered group of six. They were smiling and chatting with each other as they squeezed around the table. She could see her eyes roving over the handsome men before she turned back to her and raised an eyebrow.

"Are you sure? There is quite enough eye candy in that booth to keep a girl busy all night." Saffron twirled a loose strand of red hair around her finger, continuing to admire the view.

"Yes, I'm sure," she replied in a rush. "Which table would you like me to take in exchange?"

"Oh honey, you can have your choice." She smirked before walking over towards the group, letting her hips sway exaggeratedly.

Cordie paused as she rested her hand on the table. Her breath caught, her body flushed as a vision flashing before her eyes.

Cordie was hurt and bleeding laying on the swamp ground, where she had fallen. In her clenched hand was an amulet she had never seen before. She was trying to find a spot to hide, since she could no longer run. Her leg was sliced open from calf to ankle. Blood oozed out of the wound. She could hear them coming for her. Fear gripping her soul. She looked down at the amulet, asking for strength. The gray sapphire stone shined from within, the silver crescent moon that surrounded it was muddied from her fall to the swampy ground. A smaller gray sapphire stone hung below it, catching the light from the moon shining through the trees.

Shadows were cast looming and making it hard to discern what was real and what was not. The trees lurking above her made her feel small and intensified the fear eating at her.

She knew she had to keep the amulet safe. No matter what it cost her, she just did not know why.

Cordie sighed, as the vision faded and she focused back on the present. The heat wave fading leaving her feeling cold. Her hands were still shaky and her breathing rough. Her stomach was churning. She took a steading breath to calm her nerves. Sometimes the visions hit her hard and left her weak.

Cordie tried to interpret what the vision could mean, but nothing came to her. She felt more confused. She knew she was not going to figure it out anytime soon, so she needed to put it aside and get back to work. How much time had passed she did not know. Losing this job was something she and her family could not afford. She could try to interpret it later when she was alone.

Cordie sighed, focusing back on the present. She needed to get back to work. She could try and interpret it later when she was alone.

She looked around at Saffron's section that she had

traded for. They were all empty. No wonder she had been happy to switch stations. There goes any hope of tips for the night.

Thess smiled as Dromie came up and hugged her tight. She had missed her friend for the last few weeks. Between fixing up their house and meetings with her clan, she had been swamped.

Listening intently, she heard all the latest gossip that Dromie had. She had missed just listening to her friends rambling. They ordered cocktails, Death in the Afternoon, time to chase the green fairy around. Tonight was a night to relax and be with good friends.

She felt Kage's hand slide around her waist as he slid up next to her. His other hand holding his glass of WereWhiskey. Grif and Theo following shortly behind.

"Dromie, baby," Grif said, smiling his boyish charm at her. She huffed playfully and turned away to ignore him. "Come on. You can't ignore me forever, sweet bird."

"I believe I can, you sneaky bastard of a snake," Dromie huffed.

Thess laughed at them, knowing Dromie was slowly letting her ire with the shifter lessen.

"What can I do to make it up to you?" Grif exaggeratedly whispered in her ear. His hand snaked around her shoulders to pull her closer.

Dromie pushed him away, rolling her eyes. A smile broke across her face. Thess knew it was hard to stay mad at the charming bastard.

"Well, if it isn't my favorite halcyon," Trace purred as he walked around the corner, sliding up to the table and leaning over the back of Dromie's chair. "This oily snake giving you trouble? I can get rid of him if that is what you want. I could do it in a snap."

Trace winked at Dromie, snapping his fingers in front of Grif's face.

"You fucking blood sucking bastard!" Grif said, grinning broadly as he playfully slapped his friend on the back. "What the hell have you been up to?"

Trace laughed. "Same-o, same-o." He shrugged and pulled a chair from a nearby table up to join the group.

The waitress Saffron walked up to the table. She was a little redhead, her brown eyes sparkling with sass. "Anyone need a refresher on their drinks?"

Theo looked startled when he saw her. "Where's the other waitress?" he asked, raising an eyebrow and leaning back to peer behind Saffron.

"She needed a break," Saffron said, smiling. "What can I get you?"

"WereWhiskey," Theo muttered, frowning.

"Make that another," Grif said, raising his empty glass up before setting it down with a clink on the polished, worn surface of the table.

Trace smiled at Saffron with a cocky smile. "Can I get an Afterdark, honey?"

"I'll be right back with those drinks." Saffron winked before walking away to get their orders.

Thess looked over the dance floor to see Nem running up to them. When she got to the table, she reached her arms around her cousin and hugged her.

On her recent trips that she took to the village, she rarely saw Nem. Since there was so much going on, something was constantly preoccupying her attention. With some of the older sirens, she felt like she was running in circles, trying to make changes. They fought tooth and nail over the slightest change.

"I am sorry," Thess said. "I have been so busy I haven't been able to catch up with you when in the village."

"No worries!" Nem squealed. "So much has been changing. I didn't even have to sneak out to come here. Can you believe that? I mean, don't get me wrong, I still get plenty of dirty looks from the older sirens."

Thess laughed at her cousin while gesturing to Kage to grab another chair. "I am so happy you could come join us tonight. I have missed just hanging out with you and Dromie so much."

Saffron brought the drinks to the table, then she took Nem's and Trace's orders.

The girls sat there talking about what they had been up to these last weeks, while the guys joked around.

Thess looked up, meeting Kage's eyes. No matter how many times she saw him, he still cast a spell on her heart and took away her breath with just a glance. Her heart raced as he smiled at her knowingly.

Flushing, she turned back to the girls. Thess noticed as Nem's face softened and a blush spread across her cheeks. Just then, Nix walked up. His eyes were focused on Nem and nothing else.

Thess sighed to herself while glancing between her cousin and the witch. This was not going to end well. Nem was now looking down at her hands on the table, drawn back into her shy personality, no longer talking to anyone. Dromie, distracted between Grif and Trace's antics, had not noticed the tension between her and Nix.

Dromie continued on telling a story about her uncle Faulkner to the boys. Thess reached over and put a calming hand on Nem's hands.

Dromie turned to Nix, playfully greeting him after noticing his arrival. "I have not seen you in a while. Why haven't you been at the club?"

Nix smiled slyly. "I have been busy. Clan business."

Dromie laughed. Thess felt Nem's hand tense up and clutch her own. Thess turned to Nem, seeing the tension in her jaw as she looked down at the table.

Had I missed something? Thess thought, I have been so distracted lately.

"We should go dance!" She said, trying to distract Nem.

Nem laughed and nodded.

Gripping Nem's hand Thess pulled her onto the dance floor. She felt the beat crashing into her as she started swaying to the upbeat tempo. Nem matching the beat as they moved on the dance floor. Losing themselves in the music. It felt good to release the tension of the last weeks and just stop thinking.

After the dance, Thess pulled Nem aside before they could head back to the table. She knew she needed to figure out what was happening.

"What's going on?" Thess asked her softly.

"I don't know what you mean," Nem stammered, staring down at her feet. Trying her hardest to avoid looking at Thess.

"Really?" Thess said, her voice more stern. Trying to compel Nem to open up.

Nem, biting her lip, looked up at Thess. "It's nothing! It was at your celebration. Nix and I just danced once and…"

"And?" Thess said, calming.

"I just get butterflies around him. It's silly," she said, a blush spreading across her face. "I know Dromie really likes him and I would never want to hurt her. I swear nothing happened but a dance. Plus I doubt he would even be interested in me. He is so…"

Thess nodded, processing what Nem had told her. This was something that would create a lot of drama if Dromie knew Nem's feelings. She knew Nem would not hurt Dromie or herself intentionally. She was not sure what advice to give Nem in this situation, she did not have much personal experience with male relationships to be of help. Sighing, she hugged Nem before they walked back to join the group. Nem was acting more relaxed, now.

Thess threw her arms around Kage when they got back to the group. He bent down and kissed her forehead lovingly. The warmth she felt from that sweet kiss spread through her and made her feel at peace.

She watched as Nix kept trying to talk to Nem, and Nem would move around the table to avoid him. It was almost comical if she hadn't seen the anxiety in Nem's eyes. Her heart went out to Nem.

Theo seemed preoccupied searching around the club as well. All the while, Grif and Trace were vying for Dromie's attention. A game they played tried to one up each other for her notice.

A cold breeze wafted through the club, a chill went down Thess's spine. The roar of the music softened to her ears, as she turned to look at the doors. She felt something coming before the doors even opened.

In walked a water demon she had never seen before. His ashen blonde hair falling haphazardly over one gray blue eye. His eyes surveyed the room, filled with boredom and disdain. His pale skin made him stick out in the club. His lanky stride at the floor up as he walked away from the doors. Thess watched him as strolled around.

She felt Kage stiffen as she looked up at him.

"Is that Azazel?" She asked quietly.

"No," Kage said, sharply. "It is his son, Alistair."

Grif walked over to stand next to Kage, all thoughts of Dromie gone.

"I can take him out," Grif said, angrily. She could see the tension in Grif's shoulders. The rage in his jaw as he clenched his teeth.

"Be patient." Kage said, calmly. A calmness his body did not express. He stood rigid, ready to fight pressed up against Thess. "We will find a way to take them all down and get the amulet back. We can't just take one out, we have to do it all at once."

Alistair walked up to the bar and ordered a drink, his back to the club. Just stood there, sipping his drink coolly. Never turning around and never acknowledging them.

Thess looked over at the rest of the group. They continued on like nothing was happening, except Dromie. She was staring at Alistair's back, a look of quiet contemplation on her face. She wondered what Dromie was thinking about. She had never seen that look in Dromie's eyes before and was not sure what it meant.

Thess bit her lip, as she contemplated their next step. They needed a plan and fast to get the amulet back. Azazel could not be allowed to get his hands on any of the other amulets. There was too much at stake.

There was no more time to slide back into blissful ignorance. No more time to come and play at the club. War was coming, and they all needed to be ready.

Name/word pronunciations:

Thessalia [thes-sali-a]

Kage [kayj / cage]

Cordewai [Core-dee-way]

Thalassic [THah-lasik]

Talora [TaaL-ow-Raa]

Eldritch [El-driCH]

Helbram [heel-Bram]

Elzora [EhL-zo-Raa]

Ulrich [Uh-L-Rihk]

Amphitrite [am-fe-tride]

Cernunnos [sir-nun-nos]

Preview: Chapter One
The Clan of Luna

The forest nymph, Cordewai Grimald, flitted around from table to table, taking orders and delivering drinks. Her curly, turquoise hair floated around her like a cloud of waves. Her green eyes shined in the dim lights of the gambling den below The Wave.

Cordie had picked up an extra shift tonight. She had worked at the Den a couple of times before. The tips were nice, plus she could use the money.

There were three tables down there, fewer tables and people to tend to. The patrons usually tipped well. At least when they were winning, they did.

The bartender was out of Underdark, a sweet blood substitute. Cordewai ran up the stairs to grab another couple of bottles. Thankful to leave the watchful eye of Azazel, a water demon. She could sense he was on edge tonight. His ice-blue eyes always made the nerves bounce inside her. Her other worldly sense went haywire whenever the water demon was around.

He loomed over her in such an intimidating way. His deathly pale skin and white hair stood out in the dim light in the Den. His hair was always slicked back, exaggerating the sharpness of his features.

When she got upstairs, she decided she needed a moment of fresh air. She snuck out the back door in the kitchen.

Glancing up at the moon, she sighed. The blood ring around the full moon was a sure sign of something bad to come. Closing her eyes, she tried to mentally prepare for whatever was to come.

Standing outside, feeling the breeze, she felt the calmness settle around her. Breathing in the moonlit night air, she sighed. She needed to head back down to the den downstairs and get back to work.

When she entered the room, her eyes locked in on him. Luckily he had not noticed her entering yet. She had hoped she wouldn't have to see him ever again. The wound was still so fresh. Even after all these years, she felt that stab in her heart, her first love, her only heartbreak. Theo Deryn was sitting at one of the tables, laughing. His dirty blonde hair combed back on his head. His blue eyes sparkled as they looked at his cards. He set the cards down and his tan fingers traced them absentmindedly.

She turned away, not wanting him to know she saw him. She absently brushed her curly turquoise hair out of her face. Tilting her oval face down to look at the pad of the notepad. Her moss green eyes shining with sadness.

She stood a nimble 5'0 tall, turning lightly on her feet to go to the next table and see how they were doing.

She had put splashes of colorful eyeshadow on her round eyes, blue, green, and yellow.

She did her best to avoid his table, but as the only waitress, she knew she had to go up to it. Taking her time, she slowly made her way there. Making sure everyone at all the other tables were served first.

Staring down at her notepad, she stood at the head of the table he sat at.

"Anyone need anything?" She asked nervously.

She had not seen Theo in years. Her emotions should not be running so wild. Then, in the last month he started coming to The Wave. She had managed to avoid him every night he was in. She even debated changing jobs, but the money was too good. Her family really needed the money, so changing jobs was out of the question.

She took a deep breath, straightened her shoulders. Looking at everyone at the table but him.

Cordie was so distracted that she didn't sense the fight till it was too late. She heard the screaming of the fight, right behind her. Before she knew what had hit her. She slammed into the table as someone rammed into her back. A powerful arm reached up and grabbed her, pulling her out of the way. His arm grabbed her. She felt him press up against her, warmth spreading through her.

She saw a vision of the spell being cast seconds before she heard the male witch say the words.

Let cruelty, pain, and evil ways follow these two villians, through day and night, turn the tables and bind together these fools. I call forth the power of four, and so shall it be.

The vampire and shifter fighting behind her fell

to the ground, swinging punches, as the witch cast the spell. She felt the spell hit herself and Theo. The shock of the electric current hitting her caused black spots to come into her vision. Her lungs exhaled and she could not catch her breath.

Theo picked her up and ran up the stairs. She wished she could be happy to be out of the den, but now she was alone with Theo now. The one person she had gone out of her way to avoid. He set her down in a chair gently.

"Cordie," he whispered.

She stared at her feet, not wanting to meet those blue eyes.

Theo stood up and started pacing. She wondered if she should tell him about the spell, but couldn't find her voice. The pain had just started to recede. Her breath returned to normal finally. A feeling of hopelessness hit her. This must be what the omen on the moon had meant.

Theo was still pacing further and further away when it happened. He bounced back like he had run into a wall. He sat on his ass where he had fallen, confused.

"The witch cast a spell. We can't go too far from each other now. We are bound together until we break the spell," she said, quietly. Her heart clogging her throat made it hard to speak.

He stared at her for a moment; the words sinking in. He stood up and tried to test the boundary again. His hands hit an invisible wall. She felt the pull as he tried the boundaries, pulling her towards him. Turning, he stared at her.

"How do we break the spell?" he said sternly.

A loud crash was heard downstairs before a group of people came running out of the den, proceeding to leave through the front door. The rest being dragged out by the shifter bouncers. The night was over downstairs; it seemed, and any hope of more tips. She stared at the door they had left through. It seemed it was going to get worse before it got better.

"By having the witch who cast the spell, break it," she muttered. Knowing the witch was long gone, and they were stuck together.

Their eyes met and locked for a brief moment before she turned away. She could not stare too long in those eyes of his, almond-shaped and piercing dark ocean blue.

He started pacing again, prowling like the wolf he was. His tall, lanky strides made the space they had to feel even smaller. His firm square jaw flexed as he paced in anger. He made sure to stay close to her this time. Too close.

She stood up nervously. The jitters were getting to her. Plus, with him standing over her chair, she felt small.

"So we find the witch who did this and undo it?" he growled. His natural wolf shifter instincts coming out in his voice, his movements.

"Did you see the witch?" Cordie asked, staring at his chin. "I did not."

He sat there quietly. She glanced up to see what he was thinking. Their eyes locked as he said. "No."

For a moment, she got lost in his eyes, dark blue like a deep pool. Her breath caught as she felt something stir in her, something she thought was long dead.

She realized he had been waiting for her to look up before answering. She looked away, uneasy. Her stomach felt like it was tied in knots. How could this male still do this to her after all these years? He had broken her heart when she was sixteen years old. Eight years later, the wound still felt fresh. Obviously, she had learned no lessons, as he still twisted her up in knots.

Looking at the doorway where most of the patrons had left, she said. "We will need to find the very witch who did this to us."

She tried to use her clairvoyance to see the witch, but without much other than a spell whose trail had gone cold. Nothing came to her. She sighed and looked away.

"Well?" He grumbled.

"Well, what?" she stuttered. She needed to get her nerves under control. Why couldn't she act cool and calm? They would find the witch, and she could go back to avoiding him. Go back to pretending she didn't care.

"I know when you're doing that vision thing," he said, walking to stand right in front of her.

"So where can we find the witch?" he whispered.

"I couldn't see anything," she mumbled, staring at his chest. She felt so useless, her powers weren't strong enough yet to be able to track the spell. Plus, how did he know what she was doing, anyway? He had not seen her since the night he had broken her heart.

"Do they have a list of patrons?" He said.

Standing so close to her, he made her feel so flustered. "No," she mumbled, keeping her eyes focused on his chest. Watching his chest rise and fall fastly. He must be angry to be stuck with her. Especially when all he had wanted to do was be nice and try to keep her from getting hurt in the fight. Now he was stuck with her.

"So, where do we start?" he said, his voice lowering.

She was tempted to look up to see what he might be thinking, but kept her eyes downcast. "Weren't they your friends? Maybe you can ask around, see if they know the witch?"

He sighed deeply.

Theo stared down at Cordie, her eyes refusing to meet his. He had been coming to this club on his free nights to talk and see her. Every time she had managed to avoid him.

A month ago, he had seen her entering the club. His world had shifted. Not sure what he had hoped to gain from coming to the club. He just knew he needed to see her, to be around her. He had stood there remembering all the times he had stared into those entrancing green eyes. Eyes she would not let meet his, no matter how hard her tried to get their attention.

He looked down at her cloud of turquoise hair blowing in the air conditioning. He wanted to run his hands through her hair so badly.

Right now, she seemed so frail and tiny.. Her pale skin glowed in the dim light. He wanted to reach out and touch it, touch her.

She always seemed to avoid him when he showed up at the club, no matter how hard he tried to see her. When he sat in her section, she was all of a sudden working another section.

He had to pay the bouncer off to get her schedule for the den. It was a small place, so she could not avoid him there. He had come here tonight just to see her. She was the only friend he had in the den and the only reason he had gone down there.

"Were you hurt?" He said, gentling his voice. Her stance told him she was not happy to be stuck with him. He couldn't blame her for hating him after what he had done to her.

"No," she mumbled.

Cupping her chin, he lifted her face up. His eyes locked with hers. "Are you hurt?"

"No," she said again, with more conviction.

He nodded, letting her go.

Looking at the wall, he tried to come up with a plan. Now he just needed to find the witch he knew nothing about. Have the witch break the curse before Tala, his betrothed, found out that he was bound to another woman.

Cocktails

Please enjoy the following cocktails as mentioned in the book.

Green fairy

Ingredients:

1 fl oz absinthe
1 fl oz lemon juice
1 fl oz tonic water
1 fl oz sugar syrup
1 dash orange bitters
½ fl oz egg whites (optional for frothing)

Directions:

Add ingredients into a shaker. Mix well. Pour into chilled glass.

Death in the Afternoon-

Ingredients:

1 fl oz part Absinthe
4 fl oz champagne
1 fl oz simple syrup or sugar cube

Directions:

With an absinthe spoon or a slotted spoon slowly pour Absinthe over a sugar cube. If you don't have a sugar cube, slowly stir in simple syrup and absinthe together. Top off with the Champagne.

Pink dragon spritzer-

Ingredients:

1 fl oz gin
1 fl oz dragonfruit hibiscus simple syrup
(can substitute for another flavor)
Top off with tonic water or flavored seltzer to taste

Directions:

Pour gin and dragon fruit hibiscus syrup into a shaker. Shake well. Pour into a chilled glass with ice. Top off with tonic or seltzer water.

Ginger Gold Rush Cocktail-

Ingredients:

1 fl oz Bourbon
1 fl oz ginger liqueur
1 fl oz lemon juice
Pinch of edible gold dust.

Directions:

Add all ingredients into a cocktail shaker. Shake well.
Pour into chilled glass.

The Sea Bitch-

Ingredients:

1 ½ oz. vodka
½ oz. blue curaçao
1 oz lemon juice
Champagne to top off

Directions:

Add vodka, blue curacao, into the shaker. Shake well.
Pour into chilled glass. Add lemon juice and stir. Top off
with champagne

Stay in the loop!

Sign up for our emailing list to keep up to date on new releases, sales and more!

Follow us on our website:
AlstroemeriaPub.com

Follow us on social media
Instagram: www.instagram.com/
alstroemeriapublishing/
Tiktok: www.tiktok.com/@alstroemeriapublishing
Facebook- www.facebook.com/
alstroemeriapublishing/
Discord- https://discord.gg/eHqp9XScB4

Indie author, Krysta Lyn, is the co-writer of the fantasy romance The Calpa Series and creator/artist of the Wolf and I comic book series. An Arizona native, she is a lover of naps, cookie dough, sewing, and reading. Currently residing in the borough she lives with her husband and daughter, and is most likely multitasking. She graduated with her doctorate in advanced pediatric nursing, and practices as a full time pediatric primary caregiver. She utilizes all her free time writing, illustrating, and chicken wrangling.

Visit her social media and website to know when Krysta's next book and/or comic will come out.

Tiktok- www.tiktok.com/@FleurDeVillainy
Twitter- www.twitter.com/FleurDeVillainy
Facebook- www.facebook.com/FleurDeVillainy
Instagram- www.instagram.com/FleurDeVillainy

Johnna by day is an office worker by night writer, crafter, and baker. Her keyboard is her weapon of choice, unless in the kitchen, then it's mixing bowls. Living in the blistering sun of beautiful Phoenix, AZ. Hiking, archery, and exploring the world are some of her favorite hobbies.

Poetry is how she got her opening into writing. There, she determined to branch out into books, and is the co-writer on the fantasy romance The Calpa Series.

If you want to know when Johnna's next book will come out, please visit her social media and website.

Tiktok- www.tiktok.com/@johnna_dee
Facebook- www.facebook.com/jaydeecosplay
Instagram- www.instagram.com/johnnadeeb/